DEVON

House of Wilkshire Book 1

KATHI S. BARTON

This is a work of fiction. Names, characters, places, and incidents are products of the author's imagination or are used fictitiously and are not to be construed as real. Any resemblance to actual events, locations, organizations, or persons, living or dead, is entirely coincidental.

World Castle Publishing, LLC
Pensacola, Florida
Copyright © Kathi S. Barton 2017
Paperback ISBN: 9798891264007
eBook ISBN: 9781629898445
First Edition World Castle Publishing, LLC November 27, 2017
http://www.worldcastlepublishing.com
Licensing Notes

Cover: Linda Boulanger, Tell Tale Book Covers
Editor: Maxine Horton-Bringenberg
Formator: Charlene Bauer, Wickedly Bold Creations

DEDICATION

To the man of my dreams, my hero and my best friend. I love you so much for all that you do for me. The support that I receive and the hand holding when I need it and all the times you've let me work, just a few minutes more. My love, you are by and far the best thing that has ever happened to me. You are the champion, good guy and erotic man in every one of my books.

I dedicate this book to you for all that and more.
I love you, Paul Barton II with every fiber that I am.

TABLE OF CONTENTS

DEVON

PROLOGUE

Devon wasn't sure what he was expected to do, but stood near the grave where his father now lay. People were milling about, most of them he'd never met. Devon knew they were not there to pay their respects, but to be sure that the man of the castle was indeed dead. His father had never been someone that people would call a friend. Devon hadn't even wanted to call him father, but he'd done so. But only when necessary.

He looked out over the four graves next to his father. Women, none of them his biological mother, but women who his father had thought would replace her in some way. Most assuredly, he thought, they'd heel to him. Devon was sure that his mother had taken her last breath to escape the man who had died three days ago. But since he'd never met her, he had no idea. Her grave was some yards away, never to be associated with the man she'd married. But the castle, her legacy from a long line of her family, would be left to him now.

When someone said his name, Devon turned to look at Benshaw.

"You should come away now, sir. So that the men there can do their work." Devon looked at the men standing nearby leaning on shovels. "They've a mind to cover him up, and won't with you there."

"I'd like to see him buried. I want to see him beneath the ground, never to rise." He had no idea if anyone there knew the real relationship between him and his father, but Benshaw would. He'd been the butler in their home since before Devon was born. "Tell them to go on, do their jobs please. I want to be sure he's there when I walk away."

Benshaw nodded and moved to where the men were. When they came forward to fill in the deep hole, Devon stepped back far enough that he'd not be in their way, but not so much that he could no longer see the coffin inside it.

After the men finished — taking longer, Devon was sure, because he was there — he made his way back to the castle and the only house he'd ever known except for the boarding school. He might only be ten, but he knew that this was only a place to dwell…it had never been a home, to anyone living there. As soon as he was in the entrance hall, he looked at the man who had been more of a father to him than his real father had been.

"What do I do now?" Benshaw told him that he had a visitor. "My grandmother. She's come then."

"Yes, my lord." His new title startled him. "You will make her welcome and listen to her as if it were me speaking to you, won't you? She has a good heart."

"I can feel it. I can also feel that she has no more desire to be here than I wished to be when he lived. But stay I must." Benshaw told him to go along and that he'd bring tea. "Scones as well, please. I've not had any breakfast."

"Very good, my lord." He had no idea what the woman would want; he didn't know her either.

She'd been told, of course, that the lord of the castle was dead. Perhaps that alone brought her to see, much like he'd made sure that he was in the ground forever.

Devon went to the library. It wasn't a room he'd spent a great deal of time in. His father had told him it wasn't a place for a child. But Benshaw and the others had brought him books from it, and replaced them without his father ever knowing. Had he known, the people helping him would have been killed.

"Hello, Devon." He nodded at the beautiful woman in the chair near the fireplace. "I didn't go down because I saw no reason to disturb you. He is really dead?"

"Yes. Monday morn." If she didn't ask him how his father had come to be at the bottom of the stairs with his neck and back broken, he wouldn't tell her. "Benshaw said that he notified you right after he was taken away. Is that why you're here? To make sure that he's dead? I assure you that he is. I watched him the entire time to be sure."

"You hated him that much." Devon said nothing. There was no point. No one had liked his father, not even himself. "I won't lie to you, but I'm sure you know that I hated him as much. If not more."

"My mother. He killed her, you claimed. Father was most upset when you made those statements concerning her death." It wasn't a question but she nodded anyway. "I'm lord here now. I've decided to make a difference here and in my life. If you'd like, you may stay here. He will not bother either of us again."

"I've come to take you back with me. To my home." Devon said nothing as the tea trolley was brought in and set up. His grandmother poured them both a cup after Benshaw left them. "I have a lovely home in the States. It's nothing like this, but it is nice and you'll be well thought of there."

"This is my house now. And I am going to stay. As I have said, you can as well, but I'm not going anywhere." She sipped her tea and said nothing. "I'm nothing like him. If you come or go, that is up to you. I'm going to be a good man, and a better lord."

"I believe you." Devon nodded, putting his cup down. He'd never really cared for the drink, and now that he was in charge, so to speak, he wasn't going to be subject to it any more. "If I come here to stay, what will you require of me?"

"Require? Nothing. You are a grown woman and I don't really need you as my guardian. Benshaw and the others, they have raised me for the most part and will continue to do so should you not stay. I go to school for several months out of the year. My grades are good. I have money should I need anything. More now that there is no one to keep it from me. If you stay, I will provide for you, keep you in a manner that you should have been living before he...before his death." He thought of one thing he might need of her and voiced it. "I'd like to never speak of him again, not between us. Neither of us cared for him, as we've said, and now that he is gone, I think that should be the end of it."

"All right, I can live with that. May I bring my maid and my things?" He told her as far as he was concerned it was her home too. "Then I should like to stay. For as long as you'll have me."

Devon nodded, his body spent all of the sudden. Leaning back on the chair, he let his body relax. He thought it was the first time he'd ever felt this way in all of his life. As sleep settled over him he thought of something else. Devon was safe. Again for the first time in his life.

CHAPTER 1

25 years later

Susanna Underwood watched her grandson. He'd grown to be such a wonderful man, and she wondered more and more if her daughter would have been proud of him or would have been able to love him as she did. His father would have gone to great pains to have kept Anna from loving her son the way that she would have wanted. In fact, he had. Killing her did that.

Anna hadn't loved her husband. Not even before they were wed did she ever profess any kind

15

of affection for the man. He had been a cold man, cruel to those he had thought beneath him, which was pretty much everyone. But Anna had needed a husband and he'd been the one that had asked.

It had only taken him three weeks after the wedding to find out about the bastard child that Anna carried. Susanna had never known if he found out or her daughter had told him. But a short two weeks later, her daughter had taken a fall, and the stairs had ended the other man's child in a snap. It wasn't long after that, a few months, that Anna had told her that she was pregnant again, this time with Lord Wakefield's child.

"Are you well?" Anna had told her that she had round the clock care, that she'd been put to bed, and was to stay there so that his child would live. "I'm coming there. I want to be with you."

"Mother, I don't think that's such a good idea." Susanna asked her why. "He's not what I thought he'd be. I don't think.... He's not a very nice man. He thinks our family home should be in his name only. That it should be called Wakefield, not Wilkshire. And that's not all. He wants a boy child, Mom. If it's not, I don't know what he'll do to me."

16

"Oh, my poor child. I'm so sorry, darling. I'll come for you." She cried then and Susanna told her she was coming to bring her home. "I'll be there in a few weeks. Sooner if I can manage it."

It took her a month to get to her daughter. And when she'd arrived it was all she could do to not demand that Wakefield release her daughter from the sham of a marriage. Anna had become a prisoner in her home. Chained to the bed, quite literally, and a watchdog at her side every hour of every day.

After Devon had been born Susanna stayed by her daughter's side. She'd grown weaker everyday while pregnant, and when her son had come into the world, it had taken a greater toll on her. A short week after giving birth to her only child, her daughter had died. Susanna believed that her only child had been poisoned. Calling in the authorities had done no good. It only made the man of her family castle angrier.

After that Susanna was forbidden to set foot in the house or the property that had been in her family for generations, until the old bastard had died unexpectedly. Now she not only had her family home back, but a wonderful grandson too.

Susanna thought that Devon had gone beyond the promise he'd made to her that day, so many years ago now. He was not only a better lord than his sire had ever been, but he was a man who people simply looked up to. Devon Wakefield, tenth Marquess to the house of Wilkshire, was a man of men. And few of them knew that he was a beautiful dragon as well, just as his mother had been. Susanna's own stirred under her skin, and she had to smile when he turned to look at her, no doubt feeling her beast as well.

"You've been busy. The grounds, they're lovely." He nodded and looked out over the new gardens he'd had put in. "The orchards too. I've been to see them, and I think them coming along nicely as well."

"Benshaw loved apples and pears. I had to do something to remind me of his passing." Susanna nodded, feeling her heart break for the loss of such a good friend. "Will you be staying this time? I've had your room opened back up and aired like you like it."

"I think I shall. Will you be here as well? Or are

you going to be taking off for parts unknown again? I understand that you seldom stay put for long." He said nothing but she could feel his sadness. "What is it, Devon? You can talk to me should you need to."

"You could always read me so well. If you want to know the truth, I'm lonely. Even with all the people coming and going now, I find myself looking for someone to talk to. Benshaw will be missed." Susanna nodded but said nothing. "And a good game of chess. Have you ever picked up the game?"

"No. And I don't think I will either. You are just too good at it." He smiled at her but she could still feel his sadness. "What are you up to these days? Any more land deals I should know about?"

"A few."

Someone from the other side of the castle called for him. After asking her permission to leave her, she watched him walk away. *Such a wonderful man,* she thought again, *but so sad too. His father should have been killed long before he was for treating his only son the way that he did.*

Benshaw had taken her aside when she'd been

living there for a month. He told her that he was sure that his young master had killed his father. Benshaw also told her that, while they all thought that he'd done it, not one person in the household thought he'd done anything wrong. Apparently her son-in-law hadn't only been a monster to her daughter.

When Devon joined her again, she told him she wanted to go into town. There was much to see now, and she asked him to join her. They decided on a nice dinner, as well as a movie. A rare treat for the two of them, to be so carefree these days.

~~~

Kelly looked around her apartment once more. Everything was where it should be; the refrigerator was empty and there wasn't a bit of food, not even any canned goods in her cabinet. Her computer was packed, with every article of clothing she owned, in her suitcase. The television, long ago broken, had been put out for the trash, and she had covered most of the furniture, what little there was, with sheets. Since she planned on being gone an entire month, she didn't want to come home to a dusty mess if she didn't have to.

Her landlord met her in the hall when she came out and locked up.

"You have a good time, my dear." She nodded, almost too excited to speak. "I've got the plants you had in the windows. The mail, you said, has been stopped, and you've turned off the water to the commode as well as the sink, right?"

"I have. And I've put the lamp on a timer." He nodded. "You have your check for the rent for next month too?"

"You could have waited until you returned. I know that you're good for it. Wouldn't you have liked to have the extra money to spend on your trip?" Shaking her head, she handed him her keys. "I'll have them when you return."

"The taxi is on its way." When she picked up her luggage, all three pieces of it, he took two from her. As they made their way down the stairs, she debated on whether or not to bring up her sister and mother.

He knew them of course. It would have been hard for her to have lived there for six years and him not to have met them. Then there was the fights and police. Her family had caused her a great deal of trouble over the years. Especially her sister.

"They won't get in. I promise you that." She nodded, relieved that he'd brought it up. "And if they do get by me — and I'm going to do my best to see that they don't — you can bet that I'll call the cops again. I'm not afraid of them hurting you now that you'll be gone."

"My sister was supposed to go with me." He nodded, knowing what Rachel had done to her. "We could have had such a good time, seeing the sights and eating new foods."

"You can still have a grand time. You've worked hard for this. I want you to not think of her and enjoy this." She nodded as the tears, always there, filled her eyes. "Now don't be getting yourself worried over this. You made it work for you and you're going. Here's your taxi now."

As soon as they loaded her things in the car, she turned to Mr. Bigalow. He was one of the few people that she trusted. And liked. Giving him a hug and then getting in the cab, she pulled out a few tissues and didn't look back. Kelly was going to have fun.

Rachel had suggested this trip. A month long

vacation around the United Kingdom, a week in each country before moving to the next one. Northern Ireland first and all its rich history, then on to Scotland, Wales, then England to end up.

They'd opened a joint savings account, the first ever for either of them, and Kelly had made a plan for each of them to put a certain amount in it each week. The trip would be expensive, but it was also going to be the best money they'd ever spent. Kelly put her money in weekly for an entire six months before she checked on the progress of her sister's money, to make sure she was on track. The account was empty but for a single dollar.

Calling her sister to find out why she'd taken all her money had proven difficult. After two more weeks, with Kelly no longer putting any money in the account, Rachel showed up at her apartment, their mom as well. She wanted to know why there was no more money in the bank.

"A better question, Rachel, is why is it empty? Where is all of my money?" Rachel had waved her off, as if that wasn't important. "Rachel, I had over four thousand dollars in that account. Why did you take it?"

"I had things I needed. And the money was supposed to be part mine anyway. I just borrowed it. Also, I was thinking that Mom should go with us. She'd really like to go around the country too." A sheet of paper was handed to her. "I went ahead and made a list of things she was going to need. Clothing and things like that. You don't want her to go in her rags, do you? Also, I put some things on there you can get for me too. I put colors and sizes for us so you won't get them confused. Since you didn't put any money in the account for a while, I'm running short so you can give me whatever you were keeping out. You should help me out since it's my money too, you know."

"That money was mine." Again she waved her off. "I'm not going to foot the bill for you and Mom to go on this trip with me. It's going to be hard enough to pay for just me when you took what I already had saved."

"I don't understand what the problem is, Kelly. We made these plans, and you seem to be backing out of your part of the deal. I mean, you did really well getting that much money saved. You can do it. I'll help you." Kelly had asked her how. "Well,

24

I don't know but I'll make sure you put it in there each week like you were. And I promise to only borrow against it when I need something badly. You have no idea how nice it was to have my hair and nails done instead of just one or the other. And I needed new clothing. And Mom needed to have a new outfit or two as well. It was nice having the money around. When are you going to put more in our account?"

Kelly had said nothing. And no matter how many times her sister had asked, Kelly simply ignored her until she was leaving. Rachel finally gave her no way of ignoring her any longer.

"I don't know why you're so upset with me about the money, Kelly. It was a joint account, which means I'm as entitled to it as you are." Kelly pointed out that she'd been the only one putting money in the account. "And? I don't understand you sometimes. You act like I've wronged you somehow. Like I keep telling you, it was our money and I just used it when I needed to."

That had been over eight months ago. She'd spoken to her sister since then, but neither of them had brought up the money or the trip again. Kelly had decided after Rachel had left her that day that she was still going. By herself, but she was going, and she started to save every penny she could.

The airport wasn't very busy this early in the afternoon. Making her way to her departing area, Kelly started to get excited. She was going to be in Ireland in less than twelve hours. A whole new world was going to be waiting for her as soon as she landed, and Kelly had to sit on her hands for ten minutes before she made her way to find something to eat on the plane for the trip.

Her name being called over the intercom startled her. She thought perhaps they'd called her more than once, but she hurried to the courtesy desk to see what had happened. All sorts of things were running through her mind. She'd forgotten to lock her door and she'd been robbed already. Mr. Bigalow had fallen and hurt himself. When she was told she had a call, she took the phone with a trembling hand. Kelly had to ask Rachel twice to slow down when she started talking fast.

"I said, Mom and I are here at the airport and they don't have a ticket for us. I told them that you wouldn't have left us here in the cold, but they insisted that there wasn't one for us." Kelly wasn't sure how she'd found out about where she was and asked her. "Oh, it was on your calendar. I had to keep looking at it every time I went over to your place so I'd know. It's not very nice of you to just take off without telling us the time, now is it? Kelly, you were being extremely rude not make sure I had the right times and money for the cab ride over here."

"Rachel, I don't know what you think is going on, but I didn't buy you a ticket. I told you that you were to save for it. Did you?" Rachel asked her how she was supposed to do that when there wasn't any money in their joint account. "Precisely. I saved my own money in my own account. You would have taken that as well should I have put it in that account."

"You're being very rude, Kelly. Just give the man here your credit card number and we can meet you at the gate. I know we've gotten off on this trip a little poorly, but you'll have to get over it. I'll not have you spoil this for us because you're in a snit. Oh, and they said you didn't leave us any luggage either. You did buy the things on that list I gave you, right? I'd hate to think you left us to fend for ourselves on this trip and not have nice things."

"I'm not paying for you to come with me. You or Mom." Kelly knew that the woman next to her could hear, but Kelly was upset. "I told you when you came to my place the first time after you drained our account that I wasn't going to foot the bill. And I won't. If you have the funds, then come on through. But know that I don't have clothing for you or perfume or anything else on that list, and I certainly didn't make reservations for you to stay in the same places I'm at."

"Then we'll have to bunk up, I guess. Or you can just sleep in the chair. You know that I have that bad back. Mom can share with me." Her sister spoke to who Kelly assumed was their mother before she continued. "Mom wants to know if you got the camera she wanted. What would be the point of taking this trip if we can't take any good pictures to show off? And the man is still waiting on your card number. If you can send someone out here with it, then Mom and I can pick up a few things that you didn't get us in the stores here along the way. Kelly, sometimes I think your head isn't on right."

Kelly simply hung up, her heart hurt by the way her sister spoke to her. Making demands about things like it was Kelly's duty to take care of this. The woman at the desk cleared her throat when the phone rang again.

"She's not gonna be happy with you child, is she?" Kelly wanted to tell her that it was none of her business but the woman only smiled. "I'd go on to my gate now and let me handle this. She is a piece of work, that woman, and you worked hard for your vacation."

"I did. Months and months of going without so I could go. She watched my calendar to see when I was going to be here so she could embarrass me or something into giving her what she wants." Kelly wanted to go home...she felt as if everything was ruined now. "I don't know what to do."

"Go on back to your gate. If she doesn't have any money or tickets, she's not going to get past them up front. And if you have a phone on you, I'd turn it off and forget about it until you're in the other country." Kelly looked around when her name was called again. "Go. Sit and wait for your gate to be called. I'll take care of you not being called again by her."

When her flight was called, Kelly was almost afraid to go up and try to use her ticket. It would be like her sister to cancel her flight for her or to void her ticket somehow. Kelly was glad now that she'd put her ticket and passport in a safety deposit box in a different bank than her sister knew about. Once seated in her seat, Kelly was no less afraid. It wasn't until they were in the sky that she started to relax. Kelly was determined to enjoy this trip if it was the last thing she did.

CHAPTER 2

Devon walked to town almost daily. He could drive he supposed, or be driven, but he loved the walk. Even in the rain it wasn't bad. But today, it was simply perfect. With his dog Jamie beside him, the two of them played fetch, mostly the dog, and Devon kept an eye out for breaks in the fence.

He almost ignored his cell phone when it rang, but he lifted it from his pocket just as Jamie came back with the large stick in his mouth. Throwing it as far as he could ahead of them, he answered the phone.

"I've a favor to ask of you." Devon rolled his

eyes and thought of all the things his grandmother might want of him. He loved her, but lately she'd been making some odd demands of him. "Don't think like that. You know I have only your best interest at heart."

"If this is another set up, I'm not interested. The last one nearly had me raped." She fussed at him. "Grandma, I swear to you, if you set me up with another woman, I'm going to go back to living in the States and leave you here all alone."

"You'll do no such thing. And this isn't a date. I mean, not really." He waited, tossing the stick for Jamie again. "It's more of an escort. And not the kind that is running through that dirty mind of yours."

"Grandma, I'm a grown man. Everything running through my mind is dirty." She huffed and he laughed at her. "I'm not going to go on an escort thing either. I like my life the way it is. And if my mate, whoever she might be, comes along, then I will court her nicely, ask her to marry me, and we'll live happily ever after."

"You don't go anywhere but to town and back. Had your mate been any one of the women in town,

I'm sure you would have noticed them by now." That was the plan, he thought to himself. "Devon, I swear to you, you're making me old with this. I would like to see one of my great-grandchildren before I die."

"Do you perhaps have another grandson that is producing one for you? That would make me an uncle. I wonder, should I start knitting booties for it?" When the line went dead, he laughed out loud. "Jamie, I think I might be in big trouble when I get myself back to the house."

The walk to town wasn't just a way for him to get out of the house. Primarily it was, but today he also had business. Riley Quarter owned the local bed and breakfast, and he wanted to ask Devon about expanding. Devon was all for the idea; their little country town had become quiet the booming place over the last few years. He thought that putting in a few extra rooms might be just the ticket.

As soon as he was seated at the little bar, he was given a glass of tea. Devon would drink hot if it was the only thing offered, but most everyone knew that he didn't care for it served that way. Iced tea was his favorite drink, without lemon or sugar.

"I've got me a tenant coming in the morning. The missus is about to bust. She'll be our hundredth one since we opened. She wants to give her an extra day on us to see around the village." Devon suggested Riley see if any of the other merchants wanted to chip in on a basket and a free dinner too. "Oh yes, I like that idea, too. Something she can show off to her friends about our little town. I'll do it today. Now, business. I figure if we got out the backway some, we can add on four more rooms. Two on the top and two the bottom."

"I was thinking that you need a family room. One of the newer rooms with two bedrooms in it instead of just the one. Might make it so you don't have to double up on the rooms. You remember what happened last year when that happened?" The people had been very upset to find out that they had to share a room with their children. It had stated in the brochure that there was only the one bed, but the man and his wife thought that it meant that they'd let their kids stay for free in another room. "Those people were slammed when they gave you a bad review."

"I saw that. Made me feel pretty good to know

that so many people came to our defense." As they talked over what was going to be needed and how much money, Devon made notes. His phone had rung twice, but since he was working, he didn't bother with it. Whoever it was would either leave him a message or knew where he was to call.

At a little after two his grandma came into the little inn to have lunch with him. He was both surprised and glad that she'd done it. As they were given menus, he asked her what was up.

"Why does there need to be something up when a woman wants to have lunch with her grandson?" He just looked at her. "Oh, all right. I wanted to see if you'd please do this for me. The escort. Mary is a dear friend and her daughter is all alone."

"Did it occur to you that she might be alone for a reason?" She asked him what that meant. "That she might be tired of having someone, two busy little women, setting her up on dates, and then she has to fend off advances that she'd rather not have."

"The things you say to your poor old grandmother. Especially when she's trying to make you happy." Devon pointed out that he was very happy. "You'd be happier with a wife and children at your feet."

"Grandma, you know as well as I do that a mate for me is not in the picture. That any children that I have will be dragons. There aren't any women out there who are going to be thrilled about being mated to a great monster." He felt her pain at his words and took her hand in his. "I'm sorry. I know that relationships aren't all like the one that my father had. I know this. But in my heart, I don't think I'd be a good man to someone."

"Oh, Devon darling."

He asked to change the subject and she did. Devon hated hurting her this way, but he knew that he'd never fall in love. A woman for him was completely out of the question.

She'd driven into town on her own but he said he'd go on ahead of her, that he needed to stretch his legs a bit more. Grandma had some shopping she needed to do—a few things for her upcoming trip to see her dear friend—and she would see him at home. Devon and Jamie made their way back, both of them in a different frame of mind than when they'd started out.

"Jamie, do you suppose that she's out there?

This mate of mine." The dog woofed at him as if to say, really? "I know. It's a longshot, but I had hoped after my father was dead that I'd find her, make the house a lovely place to be, and go on as if he never was. Childish dreams, but there you have it. I was just a kid."

Devon thought of the day his father had been killed. He was pretty sure that everyone knew what had happened. Or at least most of it. Yes, he'd knocked him down the stairs. And yes, he'd not called anyone to come to his aid until he was sure he was dead. Only Devon knew what had been said between them when the fall, or in this case the shove, had happened. His father hadn't known that he was a dragon until seconds before he'd gone over.

"What do you mean, you're not human? My blood runs in your veins and I will not allow you to be anything but my heir. You will get that notion out of your head now or I shall be forced to beat it from you." He'd drawn back, as he had many times before, to slap him. "I do not want to hear another word about it. You will not change, or whatever it is you said you can do. I forbid it."

37

"I'm a dragon, the same as my mother. And her mother before her. I am dragon." The slap had taken his breath away, the pain of it taking him to his knees. His father had moved to the top of the stairs then, no doubt thinking that the conversation was finished. "Shall I show you what I am? That I can do things you never allowed my mother to do?"

He'd held his dragon to him for as long as he could. But when his father came at him again, this time with his brass knuckles on his fist, Devon had let him go. It was the dragon that had shoved the man down the stairs. He'd only been protecting him. And as his father tumbled down the long staircase, he had watched him with no emotion whatsoever. No one had even come to see what had happened until he called for them. Devon had often wondered if they, too, had waited to make sure his father was dead.

By the time Devon made it back to the castle, he was tired. He and Jamie had a light dinner and sat in front of the fireplace. It was well after midnight when he made his way up to his room.

~~~

Kelly started unpacking her things. When she'd started out on this trip she'd had only three cases...now she had four. She had spent more on things than she'd thought she would, but less on her meals than she'd budgeted out. All in all, it had balanced out. She was sure she was going to have to pay more for the extra bags on the way home, but for now she was happy.

She thought of the man who had welcomed her here an hour ago. He had struggled hard to get all four of her cases, and she'd finally had to insist that she take one. He smiled at her when they finally made it to her room.

"There's a nice wash up room down the hall. And you've a commode in here should you need it. There be no one else here right now, but we'll be full up tomorrow." Kelly thanked him. "I've made you a list of places you'd want to go, as you asked. And the local restaurants too."

Kelly looked at the pretty basket that had been in the room when she arrived, and Mr. Quarter had blustered over it for ten minutes when he told her about it. The hundredth guest this season, he'd said, and the other merchants had chipped in some of their wares as well. She was mentally making room for it in her bags when she saw the people in the streets below her. Grabbing up her wallet, she made her way out of the inn.

When her phone vibrated in her pocket she only pulled it out long enough to see who it was. Her sister had been calling her several hundred times a day, quite literally, since she'd left home. And the messages were getting more and more angry all the time. Now she only left a few words to her, mostly along the lines of she was no longer welcome to call her sister, and when she was really upset, telling her that she'd been disowned by both her and her mother. But for the last several days, Kelly hadn't bothered to even listen any more. This was her last week and she was determined to enjoy it.

The list that Mr. Quarter had given her had shops on it that she should visit. A graveyard, as well as two churches. A castle was also listed, but she was going to save that for her last day. Kelly had seen ten castles in all and had been able to explore most of them.

Making her way around the little town, she stopped in several of the shops to get herself some tea and a pretty little cup to take home. There were other things that she wanted, but she'd get them later. Now she had to get started on getting her bags ready to go home, at least the ones that had just trinkets and things in them. Perhaps she'd need to get herself one more bag. Laughing, she made her way back to the inn.

After dropping off all of her new things, she pulled her shawl around her shoulders and made her way to the first of her self-guided tours. The cemetery.

People had always thought her odd that she would enjoy a good walk through a cemetery. But cemeteries held so much history that she knew a lot about the town that used it when she left. Who the founding fathers were. Who had the most children. Sometimes she'd even find a scandal or two to keep her entertained. Most of the stories were her own, but she loved weaving them in her head.

As she entered the iron gates, she was startled to see a very well dressed woman sitting on a stone bench near a very plain headstone.

"Well, hello there. I don't believe I've seen you before." Kelly told her who she was and where she was from. "Oh, I so love the States. I was there only a few months ago. My name is Susanna Underwood, by the way. It's lovely to meet you, Kelly."

"I was just going to walk around. I won't bother you." Susanna smiled and patted the place beside her. Kelly went toward her, but she wasn't sure that it was a good idea. "This is my daughter. I come to talk to her every day when the weather is nice."

"Marchioness Lady Anna Cornwall Underwood Wakefield." Kelly looked at the woman sitting next to her after reading the name. "You're a Marchioness. A real lady."

"As are you. But we're not going to start off with you being all tongue tied about what title I have, are we?" Kelly nodded and the Marchioness laughed. "No, we can't have that. I'm Susanna and you're Kelly. I'd like to just leave it at that for the time we have together."

"I don't even think that's a possibility, do you? I mean, you're something like third in line for the crown, aren't you?" She said that her grandson was, not her. "Oh well, that makes it so much different."

"You're a treat, my dear." Susanna laughed again. "You're staying at the inn, I take it? Riley is such a wonderful man. He and his wife just opened their doors last season. I think he was surprised at how well he's done."

"I'm his hundredth guest, he said. I have an extra night to stay, but I can't. My plane leaves on Wednesday and I have to go back home." She asked her how long she'd been traveling. "A month. It's been so wonderful. I've seen so many things and eaten some pretty amazing food. One of the places I stayed gave me recipes to take home with me. I don't know that I'll try them, but I could should I want to."

"You should go up to the castle while you're here. I can get you inside of it." Kelly laughed and so did Susanna. "We should make a day of it before you go back. The place looks much better than when I lived in it, but you'll still enjoy it. And the cook can make us something special for lunch. Something foreign."

"I'd like that." Kelly knew that she was only making conversation. She knew that there was no way she'd be welcome inside the castle like she was one of them. "When I first started this trip out, I was so terrified. I had no idea what I was going to do when I got somewhere. If there was going to be enough money for me to make it. I've found some of the most generous and kind people. Some bad apples as well, but for the most part, everyone has been kind to me."

"Of course they would be. You seem to be such a lovely young woman." Kelly said nothing but could feel her phone vibrating again. Pulling it out she saw Rachel's face and put it back. "Not anyone you want to talk to?"

"No. She's upset with me and I her. I'd just soon not have to hear what she has to say to me right now." Susanna didn't ask and Kelly didn't tell her. It was too nice a day to be depressed about her sister. "I suppose I should get moving. I wanted to have a look around."

But she didn't move, only to stretch out her legs in front of her and let the warm sun shine on her face. They sat there in quiet for several minutes before Susanna spoke again.

"I miss her. My daughter, I mean. A great deal. Her husband poisoned her, I think, but I've not been able to prove it even after all this time." Kelly looked at her as she wiped at the tears on her face.

44

"I'm so sorry. It's hard when you lose someone you love very much by a senseless act. My father was murdered as well, but not by my mother. Not for lack of trying, I don't think." Kelly thought about curbing her tongue but enjoyed Susanna's company too much. "She drove him to leave home at odd hours. Just to get away from her. And one night his wanderings took him to a store that was being robbed. I don't think she ever forgave him for leaving her no one to fuss at."

"She sounds like a treat." Kelly told her that she was something all right. "You should have seen her, my daughter. Dark hair like the night. Tall like you are, and so tiny. I worried so about her when she told me she was with child. But that man, her husband, he chained her to the bed when he found she was going to have his child and ordered her not to move. I think it might have been what weakened her. Then with the birth of Devon I thought she'd be free to move about. To be what she needed to heal. But she kept getting weaker and weaker by the day until she simply died."

"You think he poisoned her, you said." Susanna nodded. "Have you had her body exhumed? I mean, there should still be traces of the poison in her body."

"Devon forbids it. He was abused by his father as well, you see, and wishes never to speak of him. Not that I blame him much. His father, as I said, wasn't a nice person." Kelly's phone vibrated again and she ignored it. "I think your sister wants to speak to you very badly. You shouldn't leave it to chance and make it so you might part with bad words between you."

"I'll talk to her later. Right now I need to get up and walk. I'm very sorry for your loss, Susanna." She stood up and took her hand in hers. "You're a very wonderful person, but I have the feeling that if you really needed to know what happened to your daughter, then you would have figured it out, correct?"

"Perhaps. But maybe I'm afraid of my grandson." Kelly shook her head with a smile. "And you know this how?"

"You have a necklace on that you play with when you're nervous or unsure that is from him. *Best Grandma* it says. I would say that you cherish it more than you do anything you've ever received before. Your watch is a man's watch, not too old, that I'm betting he gave you as well. He might not have realized there was a difference, or else he did not care because he liked it."

"The necklace is from him. Our first Christmas together." She looked down at the watch. "He gave me this when I came back from a cruise. I'd been away for a month and he'd missed me. But when I missed my connecting flight because I was delayed, he nearly went into a panic. The watch, his by the way, was his way of telling me to watch the time. How did you know that?"

"My job. I get paid to observe people. I work in the courts system in a way. I help lawyers choose their jury." Kelly looked around the cemetery. "You should give yourself some peace of mind, Lady Underwood, and either come to terms with her death or find out what you already know in your heart. But will it be worth upsetting your grandson for you to know?"

Susanna stood up and hugged her. Kelly was so moved by the gesture that she felt her eyes fill with tears. It had been a very long time since someone had hugged her for no reason. And when she was let go, Kelly wanted to beg her for just one more.

"You are a good person. And you're right. It's not worth upsetting my grandson over. It won't bring her back and it won't make me feel any better knowing that I was right." Kelly nodded. "Now, I'll call for you this week and we'll have that tour. I, for one, will be excited to see you again."

As she made her way back to the inn, she thought of the tour. There wasn't any way that she'd call, and if she did Kelly was going to beg off. To invade her home that way would be rude. And she wasn't sure what her grandson would think about a stranger in his grandmother's home. The little boy might be used to it, but Kelly wasn't.

Dinner was ready when she returned. She'd told Mr. Quarter, Riley as he insisted that she call him, to make whatever he wanted for her. She was willing to try just about anything. And when her plate was set in front of her, she had to giggle. She wasn't sure that she'd ever seen so much food before.

"It's bangers and mash." She nodded at the gentleman next to her. "Mary Margaret cooks it just right. And the onion gravy will stick to you the entire day. Even should you not want it to. Go ahead, give it a go."

The sausage was good, beef the man told her, and the mashed potatoes were perfect and not made from a box. She wasn't really sure about the baked beans that had come with it, nor the fried bread, but she tried it all. When she was finished, the man told her that she'd done well.

"I'm giving my taste buds a treat while I'm vacationing." He introduced himself as Mr. Potter. "I'm Kelly Dalton from the States."

"I thought you'd be a foreigner. I like your accent. Very lovely." She smiled at him. She had learned early in her trip that she was the one with the accent, not the people where she was. Because of course, she was the out-of-towner. When she was finished and decidedly full, Kelly decided to take another walk.

During her trip she'd walked a great deal... much more than she ever had at home. And because of that, she'd shed a great deal of weight. When she'd started out much of her clothing was in the teens, some even larger than that in size, and had been tight. Now, not only had she moved down on the weight chart, but she was wearing single digit clothing as well as feeling pretty good about herself. She had had to supplement her clothing along the way with pretty new things. Kelly hadn't felt this good in years.

When her phone went off again, she pulled it out of her pocket. Answering the call from her landlord made her smile. But as soon as she did, she knew that something terrible had happened. Kelly sat down on the small stone fence and waited for him to calm down.

"It's all gone. Everything in your apartment is just gone. I'm so sorry my dear, so very sorry." She asked him what happened. "A fire. They're saying it was set, but I don't know by who at the moment. The door to your place was broken into and the fire set was on purpose, they're telling me. I was only gone for the afternoon. I swear it."

"Mr. Bigalow, it's not your fault. I'm sure there is a good reason for it to have happened. And I have insurance on the place." Not much, but enough to cover what she might have had in the place. Closing her eyes, she asked him if anyone else had been hurt.

"No, love. We're all well. No one was home, and it was contained to your place. Only you would have asked about everyone else." He was quiet then and she asked him what else. "I hate to say this, but I think your sister did it. I saw her a few days ago, hanging around. I thought she was waiting for you to come back. She did seem to pounce on you whenever you were just getting home. But I really think I saw her running away when the fire trucks were called in."

Kelly thought of the calls she'd gotten from her. Her telling Kelly that she wasn't being fair, that she'd pay for making her miss this trip. The messages had all been deleted of course…well, except for the last few, but Rachel would never do that. Would she?

After talking to Mr. Bigalow for a few more minutes, she sat there wondering if she should bother listening to her messages. It was in her heart to say no, but she needed to know if Rachel had said anything about it. Pulling up the voice mail on her phone, she put in the code and started listening to them. By the time she got to the second one, there was little doubt to Kelly that her sister had done it.

CHAPTER 3

Devon drove through the streets carefully. He had been ready for bed when he'd gotten a call from Riley. The man was frantic with worry. His tenant had come up missing. And since she'd been new to the area, and was his hundredth customer, he was terrified that she'd give them a bad review if she got lost. So Devon got dressed and came out to find her. Jamie woofed beside him as they made their way through the rain soaked streets.

"Are you looking for her too, boy? He said pretty American. As if that were going to narrow it down." Jamie barked again. "Yes, I know. I guess she would be about the only person that we don't know, but his description was a little vague, even for him."

His lights flashed over the fence as he turned the corner. It wasn't until Jamie started barking like he saw something that he stopped. Even before he could get out of his car, Jamie had taken off. Christ, that was all he needed. His dog hurt too.

It had been raining for over two hours. Not the kind of soft gentle rain they got this time of year, but a downpour. Devon was worried that she might have fallen and the roads, which tended to flood for very little reason, might have given her a slip. When he saw the light colored clothing at the side of the road and his dog standing over it, Devon took off running.

He was sure he'd found her, but he wasn't sure about the pretty part. Her face and hair were covered in mud, her clothing was drenched, and he could see that she'd lost one of her shoes. Picking her up in his arms, he realized how slight she was and hurried her to his car. When he had the interior light on, he could see the blood on her face. Pulling out his phone, he called Riley.

"I've found her. She's hurt herself. I'm closer to my house so I'll take her there and mend her." Riley was nearly sobbing in relief. "She's breathing well and she's not hurt anywhere but a nice bump on her head. I'm sure she'll be fine."

"Please ring me should you need anything. Poor thing. I should have called you sooner." Devon thought that might have been good too as it was nearing midnight, but said nothing. "You take her on home and I'll come up to see to her in the morning. She was going to have a fry up. Mary Margaret was excited to be cooking it for her."

"I'll see you in the morning then." Putting her in the back seat proved to be harder than he'd thought it would be. She was sodden, of course, but Jamie wanted to help and he was getting in his way. Finally, he had to tell the dog to sit, and was astonished when the woman looked at him.

"Are you hurt anywhere but your head?" She just stared at him. "Miss? Are you all right? Do you hurt anywhere else?"

"I fell. I was trying to cross the little bridge and the water sucked me into it. I was afraid that I'd drown." He told her she was lucky in that. "I don't know you, do I?"

"I'm Devon. Mr. Quarter sent me to find you when you didn't come back to the inn." She nodded, then held her head. "I'm taking you back to my house to see to your head. There is a doctor there that can stitch you up if you need it."

When she fainted, he laid her back down and covered her with the blanket that was in the back of the car. Jamie moved in with her and sat very still on the floor by her head. It was the strangest thing he'd ever seen his dog do.

Driving back, mindful of the road and his passenger, Devon wondered at the color of her eyes. They were green, but not like any color he'd ever seen on a human before. As soon as he pulled under the canopy, his grandmother and doctor came out of the house. He told her he was sorry that he'd woke her when he left.

"Nonsense. I was…. Oh Devon. It's the girl from today. The one I was telling you about." He lifted the girl and took her into the house and to the clinic that was in his home. "Kelly. We never got around to her last name, but she's Kelly."

"Riley said her name was Kelly Dalton. I found

her down by the creek. She said that she'd tried to cross the bridge and the water came up too fast." Donald, his physician and friend, said he'd take care of her. His grandmother stayed in the room to help him undress her.

Jamie was sitting outside the little room when he came out. "What is it with you and this girl? Huh? She is pretty, but she's not going to like you as much as I do; you know that, don't you?"

Jamie barked and laid down. Going to his room to change into something dryer, Devon went back to wait. He told himself it was for his dog, but there was something about Kelly that made him want to make sure she was all right. When his grandma came out to tell him she was dressed, Jamie moved into the room first.

"I think he feels responsible for her. He found her." Grandma nodded and told him what they'd found. Sprained wrist, not broken thankfully. A three inch cut in the back of her head, and a few other cuts. There was some bruising on her ribs, but Donald didn't think that they were broken. And her legs were pretty beaten up. Devon could only stare at what a little soap and water had revealed.

"Pretty, isn't she?" He nodded at his grandma. "I told you she was. I worry about her though. Poor thing. I wonder what had her out in the rain like this. I hope it wasn't anything to do with her sister."

"Sister?" She nodded and told him about the call she'd not answered. "Perhaps she should have answered it. Not ignored it."

"I think there is more going on there than she said. I think there is bad blood between them. But I could be wrong." Devon wasn't sure that was ever enough reason not to talk to family. He had none but his grandma, and he needed to talk to her no matter how much she made him angry. Not that she did much, but she could be hard on a man. "We found her phone. I don't think it was damaged. It seems to work."

Devon took it and slipped it into his pocket as Donald told him what he had to do. She was going to require at least ten stitches in her head and some rest. He started on that as his grandma said she was headed to bed. He and Jamie sat with her until Donald declared her fit to move.

"I'll have her put in one of the rooms on the second floor." Donald nodded. "Do you think she'll need watching? I mean, in the event she wakes up?"

"I was going to suggest that. She's taken quiet a beating, and if she must get up in the night, or what's left of it, she might be too hurt to move on her own." He nodded and lifted her up again. "Devon, she could be taken up in the elevator."

"I have her." He cradled her in his arms as Mrs. Sounders led the way to the upper floors. Putting her in the cream room, he held onto Kelly while the covers were pulled back and the bed warmed. When he put her in the bed, Jamie jumped up on the bed with her, and he had to scold him to get down. The dog was acting very out of character today.

"You can't be on the bed with her. What if she should wake and you scare her?" Jamie whimpered as if he understood what he was saying. "Just wait until you're invited. Then you can sit by her easily. We don't want her hurting more."

When they were both settled, Jamie near the fireplace and him in the chair, Devon watched her breathing. He could not get over the color of her eyes. They were the most gorgeous thing he'd ever seen. His grandma had said they were pretty, but they were beyond that.

The room was warm and he'd been up for some time. When his eyes drifted closed for the fourth time he got up to check on Kelly and to see if she'd been chilled. Putting his hand to her forehead, he was glad to feel it warm. Devon had the most overwhelming urge to kiss her. Just her forehead, he told himself. Moving back to his seat, he let sleep take him.

~~~

Rachel watched the television. Surely this would bring her sister home. The fact that she'd not called her back, nor had she inquired about her needs, had really pissed her off. It had been extremely mean of Kelly to have not taken Rachel and Mom on her trip when it had been her idea.

"She just up and left us." Rachel nodded at her mom. "Ungrateful is what she is. And she's always been that way too. After getting our hopes up of taking this trip, she just decides at the last minute that we weren't good enough for her."

"I don't think she planned to take us at all, Mom. She didn't get anything on that list we worked on for us. And she wouldn't even put any money in our joint account any more so that I could get my nails done to be pretty when we got there. After all I've done to make this trip happen, all the things I've had to give up so that we could go? I just don't understand her." She thought of the security team at the airport that day. "Then to leave us there like she did. I swear to you, Mom, I don't know why I even try to get along with her."

"You shouldn't have even tried to do this. She went and took all of that money that she was supposed to save with you and took it all as her own." Her mom shook her head. "Then to get her panties all twisted up when you took what was supposed to be yours anyway. But I tell you, leaving us there like we weren't a part of this trip.... I just don't know if I can forgive her for that. I just don't know. We were supposed to have fun together. I didn't even get any of those new things she promised to buy me, either."

Rachel looked at the television again. They were talking about the fire like it was the only news in the world. She wanted to know when they were going to say that Kelly had to rush home. She would too. And when she got here, Rachel was going to snub her. It was what she deserved after not returning her calls.

Picking up the phone, she called her sister again. The last two times she'd called and had to leave a message, she'd been reading it off to her. It was easier and Rachel got to say what she wanted to her without forgetting anything. But when the phone was answered by a man, she sat up and felt her heart pound in her chest.

"I'm looking for my sister. Kelly Dalton. Why do you have her phone?" The man who had said hello didn't say anything. "I'm speaking to you. Why do you have my sister's phone?"

"She's been hurt. I have her in my home while she's recuperating. You must be Rachel." She said that she was and asked if Kelly had talked about her. "No, she's unconscious. Last night she fell and hit her head. Like I said, she's recuperating."

"I want to see her." The man said nothing but she could hear him breathing. "We were supposed to go on this trip with her and something happened."

"I can send a plane for you." Rachel looked over at her mom and felt like she'd just hit the lottery.

"It's about eight hours so it might be better if I just pay for you to take a flight here. That way you can be here when she wakes."

"I don't know." He said he'd pay for it and she could stay with his family. "I have our mom too. She's worried sick about Kelly."

Her mom was asking her what was going on when Rachel waved her to be quiet. This was just too good to be true. And wouldn't Kelly be so happy to see them there?

The man was talking to her and she had to ask him to repeat it. Her mind had wandered again.

"I can have tickets ready for you at the gate. You'll have to give them your identification before they'll let you pick them up. And I'll need both your names for them." She gave him that information. "Do you have a passport?"

"Do I need one?" He said that she would. "I can see. I think I have one from when Mom and I went to Canada once." That had been another trip that Kelly had messed up for them when she'd stopped putting money in their account like she was supposed to.

"All right. Let me call you back. I can arrange

to have you seats as soon as possible. Will you be packed?" She assured him that she would be and that if they needed something, they could get it when they arrived. "All right then, I'll call you back in a few moments."

When he hung up she told her mom what was going on. "So this man is gonna fly us out there with her? Well la-de-da. But what do we do about new things to wear, Rach? I mean, your sister didn't hold up her end of the bargain at all."

"I told him we'd get things when we arrived. We'll just pack what we want for now. Kelly will have to get us the things that she should have in the first place. Had she just done what she said she would, then we'd have things to wear."

Her mom went to the bedroom to start packing. Rachel did her room as well. When she had everything she thought of as nice laid out, she realized that she didn't have a whole lot. And nothing new like she'd been promised by her sister.

"Mom? I think we should take us an empty case too. That way when Kelly gets us those things, we'll have a way to bring them back. I mean, I'm all for tossing out this stuff, but she might want us to have more than we bring."

The phone ringing again had her nearly giddy with excitement. The man, Devon Wakefield he told her, had not just booked them a flight, but it was first class as well. This was much better than what her sister had planned for them.

By the time they got to the airport an hour later, Rachel had spent all the money she had on her and her mom. The things that she'd taken from Kelly's apartment, not much really, hadn't brought them much in the way of cash, but the lunch had been wonderful. And they'd both gotten their hair done with the promise of Kelly paying for it when they returned. Also a whole new set of clothing.

"She's going to have to work a lot of overtime when she comes back for this. I don't know how she's' going to manage it. But she will be happy that we finally made it." Her mom said that Kelly would really love her new blouse. "Oh yes, and these shoes. Do you suppose we should have picked her up something? She's forever pulling her hair back in one of those pinchy things. Maybe we should have gotten her one of those."

"She should have done what she said she'd

do in the first place, Rach. I mean, we had been planning and planning for this trip. And what does she do? Just acts like we didn't have any rights to be there with her. What was we supposed to do when she stopped putting money into the account that you two shared? This serves her right for breaking promises."

The meal wasn't up to par as far as Rachel was concerned. When someone was in first class they should have had steaks, not a dinner of baked sole and potatoes. There wasn't even any champagne for them. And they had to share their area with two other people. Rachel decided that she was going to complain to Devon about this; perhaps he'd do better next time.

Other than that, the trip was uneventful but very boring. And they really didn't take care of her like she thought that they should have for being who they were. There wasn't anything she wanted to watch on the television and they didn't have any way of getting anything different to watch. She asked for a blanket and was handed one in a bag rather than a nice soft one like she wanted. The bathroom was small and cramped and again had to be shared. And when she asked about sitting up front with the pilot, she'd been told no. No reason, just no. Rachel could not wait to complain about the things that she'd had to endure to her sister, because she'd not pulled her weight on their trip in the first place.

"The next time we plan a trip we aren't going to let Kelly be in charge of the money. I want the account in my name only so that she can't just take it when she wants. There is no reason for her to have stopped putting money in that account. None at all." Mom agreed with her. "And I want her to buy our things up front, not at the end. Not that she did, but she'll have to make sure that we have nice things to take with us. I bet you that she has pretty things that she got to take with her."

"I know that I keep saying this, but she's ungrateful." Rachel agreed and looked out the window. There wasn't even a good view. All she could see was clouds and nothing else. This was turning out to be the worst trip ever, and it was all Kelly's fault. Next time, she thought, she was going to be in charge of it all.

By the time they landed in England she was

exhausted. There hadn't been any beds for them to sleep in, the pillows that they'd given them were too small, and the man sitting in front of her kept scooting his seat back, and then complaining when she put her feet up on the arm rests. It wasn't as if he had been using them. The stewardess had finally told her that she was acting like she was four, and that if Rachel didn't behave she was going to have the captain land and toss her off. Like that was really going to happen. And now they were here and she was really disappointed.

"It doesn't look anything like the pictures, does it?" She couldn't see any castles, and the people drove cars around like they had at home. Even the restaurants looked like the ones that were on every street corner in their town. It was not all that special.

She stopped a man and asked him where the buses where.

"There's cabbies out front if you need one. And you can hire a limo should you want to do that. But that's expensive." She said her sister was picking up the tab on this trip. He told her where to find the limo service. "Don't forget to get your bags, too."

"Bags? I thought they just brought them to us."

Mom said that she heard someone say something about a baggage claims area. "This is just stupid. Kelly is going to have a lot to answer for when we see her. She should have told us this was going to happen. And she should have planned better. I'm telling you right now, the next time I'm going to be in charge and it will be perfect."

The baggage claims area wasn't difficult to find, but trying to remember what flight they'd come in on was hard. Finally, after finding someone to help them again, Rachel and her mom ended up at the right place and their bags were the only ones left on the carousel. Pulling them along behind them, they were headed in the direction of the limo service when she saw her name.

"I'm Rachel Dalton." He tipped his hat at her and told her that he had a car for them. "It's about time. You should have come in here and helped us with these bags too. Kelly should have told you that we would need extra help. We're her family, after all."

The drive over was quiet. Rachel had asked the man for some music and he said that the car hadn't been equipped with any, that the household didn't like it when they rode. That was by far the dumbest thing she'd ever heard and told him so. The glass between them went up when she told him she was going to tell Kelly what a shitty job he'd done for them.

"Christ, everyone is so rude any more. Kelly certainly has a lot to explain when we see her. I think she'll have to buy us something really nice when we get back. Perhaps she can buy one of those big screened televisions. That would be a good start."

"I was also thinking that we should just move in with her. That way we can know firsthand when she's working and getting ready to leave us again. She also has that nice laundry room. It would be so much easier for her to just wash our few things with hers. I hate going on the bus to do our washing." Rachel loved that idea. "And grocery shopping. What's the point in us buying for two houses when she can just pick up things that we like with hers? Maybe we can have her get cable with all the channels, too."

"She only has the one bedroom, though. You and I will take that, of course, and she can take the couch. There are two of us, and the living room will be cramped for two people." Her mom nodded. "She won't mind going out when we want to watch something on TV. Or we can work out a schedule for her to work late on those nights. And the extra money will be good too."

The trip might have started out badly, but things were falling into place now. They would all live in Kelly's apartment, and Rachel and her mom could use their money on things that they needed. It wasn't like Kelly dated, and she was too fat for most men to find attractive. Rachel told her all the time that men didn't like heifers. And that was what Kelly was. A big old fat girl with pretty eyes.

When the limo pulled into the drive, Rachel started to knock on the window to ask where he was taking them. Then the castle, an honest to goodness castle, came into view. She looked at her mom and they both squealed. They were going to be staying in a castle.

CHAPTER 4

Kelly opened her eyes and saw the man sitting in the chair. Before she could move and figure out what was going on, a soft snore had her turning. The big dog laying against her backside made her smile. Kelly had a weakness for Irish setters. When he opened his eyes and looked at her, Kelly simply fell in love.

"Hello boy. What's your name?" She found the beautiful collar around his neck and read his name. "Well, hello James, my name is Kelly. Do you happen to know where I am?"

"My home." She turned to look at the man who

hadn't moved other than to open his eyes. "I call him Jamie. For some reason he's taken quite a shine to you."

"He's beautiful." Almost as if he knew she was talking about him, he licked her face. The pain of it had her moaning.

"Come on, boy, before you hurt her again." The dog leapt off the bed at the man's command and she tried to sit up more. "You feel all right? Do you need anything for pain?"

"No. I think I'm fine." He nodded and still hadn't moved. "I think I remember you, but I'm not sure. I fell and you found me."

"Yes. The creeks around here swell quickly, and if you're not careful they can pull you in. Mostly it's smaller items, but on occasion a dog gets pulled in. How are you?" She told him again she was fine. "I'm stalling. I have made a mistake, I think, and I don't want to tell you about it. You'll find out sooner or later, but...well, sooner I guess, but it's been something that I've regretted since they arrived."

"I see." He sat up now and she could see that he was incredibly tall. "Maybe if you tell me what it is you've done I can help you with it. I'm pretty good at figuring things out."

"I had your things brought here from the inn. Riley's been to see you, by the way, and is feeling better about losing you when he did. I don't think it was his fault, but he did blame himself for giving you the list." She tried to keep up with what he was saying, but he kept jumping around with things. "I'm Devon. I told you that before, but you might not have remembered. And you're Kelly Dalton, from Ohio."

"Yes, I am, and no, I didn't remember your name. What did you do wrong?" He grinned at her and she felt herself warming to him. Even though he was a little odd. "Am I not going to like it?"

"I don't think so. You seem pretty normal. And my grandma had claimed that you're nothing like them." She asked him who he was talking about. "My grandma...you met her in the cemetery that day. She said that she invited you to have a seat with her and that you were so sweet. It's one of the reasons I think you might be adopted."

"I'm not. I wish it at times, but...why would you think I was adopted?" She heard voices in the hall and looked at the door, then back at him. "You didn't. Please tell me that you didn't bring my sister here."

"I'm afraid that I did. And your mom. I thought it would be a nice treat for you." She lay back on the bed again. "They're not very nice, are they?"

"No. They're rude and mean at times." She had no idea why she felt she could tell him that, but she felt the weight of her family crush her. "Where am I, and is there a back door to escape?"

He laughed. It was full of life, but she had a feeling that he didn't do it often. It took him by surprise too, she'd bet. When he stood up she watched him walk toward her. And when he sat on the edge of the bed, she felt heated by his closeness.

"My name is Devon Wakefield, tenth Marquess to the house of Wilkshire." Kelly nodded as he lifted her up from the bed and put her on his lap. "And as such, I'm the lord of the castle. A castle that has been in my family for ten generations. A castle that hasn't known happiness for a very long time."

"And you thought my mom and sister could bring you that happiness? I'm sorry to tell you this, but they only bring grief and sorrow." He said that he'd discovered that too. He pulled her hair from her neck and she nearly moaned. "Is there a reason that you're holding me like this? Not that I'm not enjoying you...it, but I don't know you."

"No, you don't. Not yet, at any rate." She felt his breath on her neck and her nipples tightened. "You're something else. Not at all what I expected. It took me a while to figure it out, but now that I have, I find that I'm quite happy with the results."

"I see. Actually, no I don't. Would you mind not speaking in riddles and tell me what the hell you're talking about?" He kissed her throat, then her chin. "Devon, you're making me all hot and bothered, and I don't think you've explained to me what's going on, why my family is here, or for that matter why I am in your arms."

"I answered your phone when your sister called. I brought them here because, and I see this as my mistake now, I thought it would be nice for you to recuperate with them here. They aren't the sort one calls when you're ill. May I kiss you?" The change of subject caught her off guard, and she was nodding about her sister when he pulled her mouth to his.

This was no simple meeting of the lips. She felt devoured by him, consumed by his heat. And when he shifted her on his lap, Kelly felt herself being touched in places that seemed to beg him for more. His hands were everywhere, his mouth moved over the same path. And when he took her bared breast into his mouth, Kelly held him to her, curling her fingers in his hair.

"You taste like I thought you would." Kelly wanted to ask him why he'd been thinking of tasting her when she felt him between her legs, his thick cock at her nether lips. "If you were to come right now, would the household hear you scream? Would you cling to me while I feasted on your body?"

"I've never had sex before." He chuckled and told her he knew that. His mouth was at her belly, his tongue in her navel. When he sucked hard on the indentation, she cried out and wrapped her legs around his. "What are you doing to me? I don't think we should be doing this, do you?"

"Oh yes, I very much do." Looking down her body at him, she realized that she was naked, that at some point he'd laid her out on the bed and had stripped her naked. She watched him lower his mouth to her pussy and cried out again when his tongue teased her clit. "I'm going to eat you. Then if you'd like, I'd very much like to come deep inside of you. Would you like that as well?"

"Yes."

He covered her mound with his mouth and she felt his teeth nibble at her clit again. His hands were holding her; his mouth was doing amazing things to her. And when he bit down on her, his fingers sliding into her pussy, Kelly felt herself bow up off the bed as the most incredible pleasure washed over her. Grabbing the pillow by her head, she screamed out her release as he continued to feast on her.

He didn't stop. Devon made her come a dozen or more times before she begged him to please let her rest. But when he sat up on his knees between her legs, she could see that he'd stripped too, his body bared for her to see him. And Christ, what a body he had.

"I want to come on you this way the first time. My need to claim you is beyond what I think you can handle our first time together." He wrapped his hand around his leaking cock and moved it up and down. "Do you have any idea what I want to do to you?"

"Fuck me?" He laughed and said yes. "I'd really like to feel you fucking me. I mean, I've never done it before, but I have a feeling that you'd be really good at it."

"You're making it very hard for me to be a gentleman about this. I wanted us to go slowly this time." She realized he'd said that before and asked him about it. "Do you want me? Right now? Or do you want me to explain things to you? I can do that, but I think we'd both enjoy this more."

"You're stalling again." She watched as a thick cream leaked from his cock. "Will you explain as soon as you're done with me?"

He moved then, his body stretching out over hers. Kelly felt her pussy soak and her body tighten at the thought of him taking her. But when he touched his mouth to her nipple she held him there and begged him to do it.

"I will, but I want you to enjoy it as well. Relax, darling. I won't enjoy this if you don't." She tried to relax but she was sort of nervous. "You have the most beautiful body. And I love the way your nipples tighten when I touch my tongue to them."

He did that now, his tongue teasing the very tip of her breast. And when he nibbled on her, Kelly wrapped her legs around his thighs and felt his cock at her entrance. She tensed up again.

"Just do it." He laughed again. "I'm afraid you won't fit or something. I mean, I know how sex works, but you're really big."

He thanked her. "I can't *just do it* if you're too tight, sweetheart." She had a feeling he was teasing her, but he spoke again before she could ask. "The thought of sliding my cock into your heat, your wet body, makes me want to come right now." As his cock touched her, gently moving in and out of her, she began to need more from him. Rocking up when he pulled back, he moaned when she did, and she wanted to beg him to take her. "Come for me, Kelly. Soak me with your juices and I'll fill you."

Her body did as he said like he'd pulled a string. She screamed out her release, feeling it all the way to her toes. But when he moved into her, she felt like he was tearing her apart and held him still.

"It's too much. I'm so sorry." He kissed her and

she looked up at him. "You can just go if you want. I'm okay. You gave me so much before this."

His body moved. There wasn't any more pain but the most wonderful pleasure. Begging him to do it again, he lifted her ass up to his body and she wrapped her arms around his shoulders. He moved slowly, filling her with his cock, and she wanted more, needed more. When he kissed her again, this time fucking her hard, she held him as tightly to her as he was her. And when he bit down on her throat, his teeth pinching at her flesh, Kelly came so hard that she literally saw stars dancing behind her eyes.

"Again, love. Come for me again." She cried out when he held her to him, his body pounding hers in a way that she thought that she'd come apart, but the pleasure was building again and she had a feeling this was going to be better. "Take me into you. Drink what is freely offered. Take me to your heart."

She wanted to ask him what he was saying, beg him to repeat it. But he pulled her mouth to his throat and told her to drink. The first taste of blood, hot and spiked with something delicious, had her craving more. Sucking on the wound at his throat, Kelly screamed again when he tore at her own throat and filled her. She came hard and was dizzy with it. She felt the moment that he released too, felt his cum as it filled every part of her. Darkness swallowed her up and she didn't think she'd ever come back from it.

~~~

Devon held her to him. He hadn't meant to go this far with her, but Christ, she was beautiful and he'd not been able to resist her. When she stirred, he looked at her face and wondered why he'd been so afraid of having someone in his life and had tried too hard to avoid it. He smiled at her when she opened her eyes.

"We had sex." He nodded, feeling like a fool laughing at this. "I don't think we should have done that, do you?"

"Oh. Did you not enjoy it? I could try harder if you'd like. I'll have to wait for a couple of minutes though…you wore me out." She smacked his arm. "You are so beautiful."

"I'm not, but I thank you. And so you know, you're supposed to woo a woman before you take her to your bed. After sort of defeats the purpose of it. I mean, we already did it." Kissing her again, he felt her body move against his. And when he lifted his head from hers, she looked dazed and as needy as he felt. "I'm thinking that once was not enough for you."

"No, but I can wait. You're going to be sore enough as it is." Her face reddened and he had to laugh. "Would you like for me to run you a bath? I could wash your back. We could even have a little fun while we're at it."

"You said that you would explain things." He nodded but kissed her again. This time she jerked his head up and glared at him. "Explain."

"All right. I brought them here because I felt badly about your being hurt. Your sister...well, I must confess that I had thought to mend any broken fences between you. My grandma said that you'd not taken her call, and I was under the assumption that I would help you. I should have stayed out of it." She said that he should have. "Okay, what else do I need to explain before I can make love to you again?"

"You're a Marquess. Of a castle." He nodded,

and felt hurt that her voice sounded so sad. "I'm a woman from Ohio that hasn't two pennies to rub together other than the little cash I have to go home on. I have less than that. My apartment caught fire and I have nothing at all now. We shouldn't even be in the same zip code, much less in bed together."

It was on the tip of his tongue to tell her that she had all she wanted, but he felt that she might hurt him. He watched her face as every emotion she had moved over her. He needed to have a talk with her. Should have before he took her. He held her to him as he tried to think how to begin. The start, he supposed, would be the best.

"I'm not sure how much you know about non-humans." She didn't say anything and he moved forward. "I'm not human. I know that's blunt, but I want to tell you about myself. I need you to understand that I wasn't looking for you when I found you, but now that I have, I need you in my life."

"What do you mean, you're not human? And I know a few shifters. Are you saying that you're some kind of shifter?" He said that he was. "And this thing here, this sex between us, you needed to

85

score with a woman and figured I'd do? This guy I know, he told me that to fuck humans is the best. There would never be a child to come back to haunt you."

"No, it's not like that." He watched her when she got out of the bed, wrapping the duvet around her. He nearly begged her to come back to him when he saw his mark on her. "You're my mate, Kelly. I knew it the first time I touched you, but I was too worried about you to know what it was. See? You have my mark now. It's there on your hip."

Adjusting the blanket, she looked down at her hip and he sat up on the bed. Kelly stared at it for several seconds, not saying a word, before she sat down on the chair he'd been in the last three nights. When she only stared at him, he thought perhaps she was in shock and started to ask her if she was all right when she spoke.

"That is a dragon on my hip. And it wasn't there before." He said because they'd not had sex before. "Don't be a dick. I'm dealing right now."

"I'm sorry. I'm trying to help you." She snorted at him and he wanted to laugh. He wondered if she'd hurt him if he told her he was enjoying this more than he had anything in a long while.

"So this dragon on me. I'm to assume that because you say we're mates — not that I'm saying I believe you, but you say this — this is why I have a dragon on me."

"Yes. When we find our other half, our mates, we share a mark. Mine is a green dragon. Like the one on you." She didn't speak but sat there staring at the wall beside him. "Can I continue to explain?"

"Not yet. I'm processing." He pulled the blanket over his legs and watched her. He could have dressed himself, her too, but he was worried that might be too much for her. "Explain to me why you thought it would be a good idea to bring my sister and mother here. And so you know, you're going to regret that more and more before we leave here."

"You can't leave me. Well, you could, I guess, but I'd follow you. And I'm not sure I could regret them more. They're very...manipulative, aren't they?" She told him he had no idea. "I'm beginning to see that. Rachel told me about the joint account and how you didn't hold up your end of the bargain you'd struck. That's when I discovered that she doesn't hear what she doesn't like…or pretends to not hear. And after you stopped putting money in it you had the nerve to get pissy, I think she called it. She doesn't understand why you didn't do anything you promised her. I'm assuming that you made no such promises. Your mother told me how you'd left them at the airport without any tickets to travel with you when it had been Rachel's idea. Not a ticket nor any new clothing either, she said. I found the list in your things when I was trying to find your clothing size."

"Why did you need to find my clothing size? Never mind. I'm sure they told you what an ungrateful daughter and sister I am too." Devon nodded. "I'm assuming that at some point before we had sex you had an idea who I was to you. Or who you think I might be to you. How did that come about?"

"May I show you?" When she hesitated, he slid off the bed and made his way to her on his knees, speaking low as he went. "You were battered pretty badly when I found you. Sprained wrist, a gash in your head. There were bruises too, along your legs and ribs. Donald, my physician, said that he thought that you'd not broken anything, but he wasn't sure."

"The water. I was watching the rain coming over the mountains. I saw the castle then. And I wasn't really paying attention to my surroundings. The little bridge I was standing on...the creek beneath it filled to overflowing in a matter of seconds." He nodded and took her hand in his. The one that had been hurt. "I'm not hurt. You fixed that, didn't you?"

"Yes. As soon as I touched you after I realized who you were, my fingers running over the wound, you were healed. For some reason...I don't know why, but I guess I had to acknowledge you in some way as to who you were. The marks to your skin were gone, the swelling in your wrist disappeared as well. It was as if you had never been hurt." The noises at the door had them turning to it.

He knew it was her family. They'd been trying to get in since they'd been brought to the house. Devon was sick of dealing with them and had only been doing so because they were Kelly's relatives. When she said his name, Devon looked at Kelly.

"I guess I have to go and see to them." He

told her they would. "They're my problem. And as much as I hate to say this, I really wish that they were someone else's. I never realized until I took this trip and made decisions based on what I wanted and needed how much they were dragging me down. I don't know what I'm going to do when I get home."

"This is your home, Kelly. Anything and everything that I have, it's yours as well." She shook her head and he grabbed it in both of his hands. "It is. You are my mate. My one and only love. You are, as of the moment we made love, the Marchioness of Wilkshire."

Her mind worked around his words. He could see it, almost feel it beneath his hands. And when she smiled at him, he was sure he was going to love whatever she came up with. Devon was very glad that it wasn't going to be directed at him, whatever she'd come up with.

"You brought my clothing here?" He nodded and put his hands on her arms and dressed her. When she inhaled sharply, he apologized. "Don't do that...that was amazing. But don't do it again without some warning. By the way, can you do that to anyone?"

"No, just you and I." When she stood up, he dressed as well. "I must say, you are beautiful naked, but positively gorgeous dressed as well."

"You, my dear dragon, are a charmer." She went to the mirror and then looked back at him. "This is really pretty. I saw this...in one of the shops when I was traveling. How did you...? Can you read my mind?"

"And you can mine as well." He sent her an image of her riding him. "I'd very much like to strip you down again and have you sitting atop me."

She helped him stand and kissed him quickly before going to the door. "First we have to deal with Rachel and my mom. Then we can spend the day in bed. After you tell me everything else. I'm not saying that I'm ready for it all, but I'm getting ready to listen."

"Are we tossing them out? I can have Benshaw help." She asked him who that was as she stood at the door with her hand on the knob. "Benshaw, a man I admired and loved more than anyone else, died a few months ago. He was my friend, butler, and ran the household. His grandson, also

Benshaw, has filled his shoes. I think you'll like him. Are we going?"

"I'm afraid." He moved up behind her and wrapped his arms around her waist, and Devon was glad when she leaned back against him. "It's not going to be easy or pretty. But I'm tired of them."

"I'll be there for you." With a short nod, she pulled the door open and stepped into the hall. Devon smiled and followed. He'd hate to be her sister and mom right now.

Chapter 5

Rachel looked at the woman coming down the stairs, and it took her several moments to realize it was her sister. Christ, what did she do to herself? When her mom came around the corner from the kitchen, Rachel pointed to Kelly.

"She's had work done. I guess she wanted to be more like me." Mom nodded and she looked at her sister again. "I was wondering when you'd figure out that you needed to get some lipo done. Good job. But don't think I'm any less upset with you. You ditched us when you made promises to me and Mom."

"How is it that you feel I slighted you when all I did was take my money that I earned and went on a trip of a lifetime? And so you know, I didn't have lipo done. I got out and had some fun. Without you. It was invigorating too." Rachel wasn't sure what that meant so waved her sister off. "When are you going back?"

"I've set up some things for you to get for us in town. One of the shops even said they'd send it home for us if you didn't have room in your bags. And there is this place where we wanted you to take us for dinner tonight. We'll need something new for that." Kelly said no and walked by her to go to the kitchen. "One of the places said they'd need a deposit to hold things so I told them I'd tell you today to pay it off instead."

When she entered the kitchen behind Kelly, everyone was standing up and looking at her. She knew it was their lunch time; they'd told her they weren't going to help her with a snack because of it. Now they looked like they were going to stand there all day for some reason.

"Please go back to what you were doing. I just came in to get something to drink." Bento, or whatever his name was, said he'd get it for her. "Thank you, but I can do it. I don't want to disturb your meal."

"It's fine, my lady. While you are here, I should like to introduce you to the staff. And to see what changes you'd like to make."

Rachel laughed and they all turned to her. "First of all, she isn't anything close to being a lady. Kelly is just a person like me. Not as pretty, but she's no different than I am." The people continued to stare at her. "I'd like that snack now, too, if you're fixing something for her. Some fruit too, not that kind you made yesterday. It's not fit to eat."

"My lady?" They all turned to her and Kelly smiled. Bento left the table and poured a glass of tea for Kelly and then sat back down. The rest of the table did as well. "This is Mrs. Bevel. She's the day cook. Mr. Bevel takes care of the gardens, as well as the new orchard. Then there is Miss James. She's the lady's maid for Lady Susanna. We'll have to do some interviews for yourself one soon. And then there is—"

"Kelly, I need your credit cards. Mom and I have things to do, and you knowing who these people are is boring and has nothing to do with what I want." Kelly turned to her and Rachel took a step back from her. There was something there, a power or something, that scared her a little. "Mom and I are making up for what you did to us when you just left us at the airport. We didn't get to go all over the place because you didn't hold up your end of the bargain."

Devon came into the room then and the people at the table stood again. It was like having a jack in the box or something. But when he waved them to sit, they did. Kelly handed Devon her half glass of tea and the man actually kissed her. Before Rachel could comment, not even sure what she'd say, Kelly spoke.

"I'm not going to give you any money. You're not going to have things shipped home unless you've paid for them. There won't be any dinner out tonight, again, unless you're paying for it." Rachel just snorted. Her sister was forever saying things like that. She never followed through with it, so she wasn't sure why she even bothered. "I'm not kidding you, Rachel, I'm finished."

"All right. If you say so. But when are you

going to give me the cards? I have a lot of shopping to do before we can go back. Oh, and when you get our tickets for that, make sure you get the two seats in front of us, too. I don't want anyone cramping me up when they need to put their seats back. Mom and I had a miserable time. And you know what, they didn't serve steaks either. How hard is it to throw a steak on the grill, for Christ's sake?"

"You were in first class. I'm pretty sure that's about as much room as you can get on a domestic plane." Rachel decided that she didn't care for Devon very much. He was rude and hadn't been doing a thing for them. "But it matters little. I've made arrangements to have you taken back on Monday. My plane has a great deal more room in it, but you still won't get a steak on the grill. First of all, you're about thirty-thousand feet up, and cooking is prohibited in planes."

Whatever, Rachel thought. She'd talk it over with Kelly later. She'd make it happen. Kelly still owed her the money she spent on the trip that her and Mom didn't get to go on. Rachel reminded her again about the credit cards.

"I'm not giving them to you. You're not going

to get anything from me again."

Rachel left the kitchen. She was showing off, that was all. It was just like Kelly to try and make her look stupid in front of strangers. Rachel made her way up the stairs to just get the credit cards when she was stopped by the man that had been outside Kelly's door when she'd been taking a nap.

"May I help you?" Rachel ignored him and went to the door. It was locked. "Lady Kelly is downstairs, miss. If you need anything from her, she'll have to get it."

"She has the credit cards in here and I'm here to get them." He didn't even move. "Come on and open this door. I told Kelly I needed them, but she's down there showing off. Just open the door and I'll get what I need."

"That's not going to happen." She cocked a brow at him. "When Lady Kelly wants you to have something from her rooms, she'll — "

"Why are you calling her *Lady* Kelly? She's not *lady* anything. Just open the damned door so I can go into town. And the big car will be fine for us to use. I have a lot of things I need to pick up." Again, he just stood there. "This is getting ridiculous. Just give me the key and I'll open it. I have shit to do."

When he just turned and walked away, Rachel decided that she'd had enough of these people. Kelly never did what she needed her to do lately. She knew how much she needed to get those things paid for. And Kelly owed her, damn it.

Standing back, she kicked at the door. It didn't even move, so she hit it twice more before she was knocked down. And when she tried to stand up, the man over her told her to be still. Devon. She should have known he'd be sticking his nose where it didn't belong.

"What the hell do you think you're doing?" Rachel tried to look at Kelly, but the man was holding her down. She wanted to know what he thought he was doing as well. "Why were you trying to break down my door?"

"The credit cards. Damn it, Kelly, I told you to get them and you just had to show off. This is like that stupid money in our account. You acted like I had no rights to any of it when it was my account too. Just tell him to get off me and I'll just be on my way." No one said anything, but she did see her sister open the door. "Finally. I'll need cash too if you got any on you. If not, I can just get an advance on your card. You should learn to carry a lot of cash around for things like this."

When Kelly returned she sat on the floor in front of her. She had the cards now and Rachel thought of all the things that she and Mom had put on lay-by. She decided to get a couple of pieces of extra luggage too while she was out. But when Kelly started cutting the cards up, Rachel asked her what she was doing.

"Ending this thing you have about my cards. They're maxed out anyway, so you wouldn't have been able to use them once you stole them from me." Rachel started to tell her that she'd never stolen anything in her life. "Oh really? What about my money out of the account? What about the time you came into my place, took all my shoes, and sold them? Or the time that you took my computer out of my place and sold it too? And let's not forget that you broke into my apartment the other day and set fire to my bed."

"So? I don't understand you sometimes, Kelly. It's like you don't listen. I'm not going to say this again. It was our account. Our money to go on a trip that you decided at the last minute to take all the money and go on your own. Christ, you'd think that burning your things was that big a deal. It was shit anyway. And I wanted you to come home and get us. You promised us a vacation, new clothing, and a good time. You didn't do any of that for us."

Kelly sat there. Rachel jerked free of Devon and stood up. Taking the pieces of the credit card from the floor, she tried to put them back together. There was still enough there to see the numbers, so it might be fine. Making her way down the stairs again, she told Mom that she had the money now. They were going to get some really lovely things despite Kelly being a bitch about it.

~~~

Kelly felt like she'd been drained. Rachel would never see things any way but the way she wanted to. She looked at Devon when he sat across from her. And when he took her hands into his, she smiled.

"She's going to be in for a big surprise when she tries to use those. They really are at the limit." He stood up and pulled her from the floor with him. "I'd really like to go back to bed with you. Do you think that would be all right?"

"Absolutely. But I have to make a phone call first. Do you want to go to my office with me?" She nodded and walked down the stairs, holding his hand. "Benshaw is appalled, by the way. So is the staff. Not at you, but that your mom and sister treated you that way. I assured them that they'd be leaving soon. I was wondering if you'd stay here and marry me."

She stopped moving about halfway down the stairs, and he turned and looked at her. "Marry you. You just said that you wanted to marry me." He nodded. "You don't know me that well. Not to mention...you do remember meeting my family, right? If I say yes, and I'm not saying I will, but they'll be related to you too."

"I'm not worried about them. Once they're gone then it'll just be you and I here. I have a feeling that they'll never save enough for one of them to come back, much less the two of them." She started down the stairs again. He had a point. "You'd have to do me a favor though. It's not a big one, but I'd like for you to let me show you what I am."

Again she stopped and he turned again.

"You're a dragon. And you want me to see you. I need to sit down."

Sitting on the stairs, she squeaked when he picked her up in his arms. "At the rate that we're moving to my office, we'll never be there in time. I have to make a call about your family."

She sat on his lap when he picked up the phone. It was one of the old ones with a rotatory dial, which she teased him about. When he spoke on the phone, she leaned on his shoulder. There was something about this man that made her feel safe.

"Yes, this is Lord Wakefield. Thank you. There are two women coming into town soon, if they're not already there, that may try to set up some arrangements for this house to take care of some billings. I have not authorized them. Nor will I pay for any damages should they create a scene." He paused and then looked at her. "I see. Yes, I can understand that you needed to take quick action. If you'd be so kind as to hold them for a few hours, I'll be down when I can make arrangements to have them flown home. Thank you very much for helping me out with this."

When he put the phone back in the cradle she

wasn't sure she wanted to know. But when he lifted her head up and looked her in the eyes, she could see the humor there. Whatever had happened had make him laugh.

"Your sister and mother are in the local jail. Both of them, apparently, are demanding that they be freed this minute and you be arrested. You have given them stolen cards, it seems." Kelly nodded. "What did you do?"

"When I found out that Rachel burned my apartment, I canceled all my cards. I wasn't sure if she'd found my statements, which have enough information on them to give her some use of them. I'd been meaning to cut them up, but I've been... distracted." He turned her on his lap so that she was facing him. "I thought we were going to go back to bed."

"We will. But I can play here as well." Her buttons were undone and then her blouse taken off her. "I can strip you as quickly as I dressed you if you'd like. Both of us can be naked right now if you'd let me."

"Do it." She felt his cock at her pussy. His hands were at her breasts as he took them to his mouth. Sitting up enough to slide over him, she rocked forward. "Don't hurry. I need this. I want to feel this for a long time."

"Forever if you say yes to my question." Her mind was too full of lust to think what he was talking about. "If I set you on the desk, I can eat you until my heart's content, love. Would you like that?"

Her nod had him lifting her and sitting her in front of him. She felt exposed this way, but he pulled her legs apart when she started to close them. Laying back, she felt his tongue at her clit, and when he slid his fingers inside of her, Kelly nearly came up off the desk.

"Come for me, love. I want to drink all of you while you ride my fingers." She cried out when he suckled her clit into his mouth and bit down. The more he fucked her this way, touching off more nerve endings than she'd known she had, the more she needed from him.

Even as he ate her, his hands were everywhere he could reach. Her breasts were cupped, her nipples tugged on. When she came, twice in a row, he begged her for more. His voice in her head was soft, demanding, and loving. Every time she came, each release seemed to fill her with a need that she knew that this man would quench. And when he stood up, she watched him as he fisted his cock over her.

"Christ, do you have any idea how much I love you already? All I can think about is waking next to you every day. Making love to you whenever I need you. Growing old with you, having children." Kelly felt her breath leave her as he slowly entered her. "So tight, so wonderfully wet. Come for me, love. Come for me and let me taste you when you do."

He leaned over her, his body a part of hers, his cock filling every part of her. When he kissed her, tangling his tongue with her own, she could taste herself on his mouth and wanted it all. Pulling his neck to her mouth, she nipped at his pulse there. It was pounding and hot, blood just there on the surface for her to take. When she bit him, sank her teeth hard into his flesh, she was rewarded with the sweetest taste she'd ever had, his blood filling her mouth.

"Come." She did, her body no longer hers but

his to command. And when he roared out, biting her as she had him, Kelly knew then that she loved him and would do so for the rest of her life.

Devon held her to him. And when he stood up, she had to work hard to make her limbs hold onto him as he sat them back in his chair. Both of them were breathing hard and she felt like she'd been drained. Tremors shook her, small climaxes that made her shudder with every release. Christ, it was like having her body put into an electrical socket and someone was playing with the switch.

"I love you." He lifted her chin up to look at her and asked her to say it again. "I love you. I have no idea how something so profound can hit you so quickly, but I do love you."

"And I you." Suddenly she was dressed and so was he. As they made their way to the back of the room and the large doors there, she had a glimpse of a pool and another house before they were standing in the yard. "Are you ready?"

"For?" He grinned, and then...he was simply gone. And in his place was a big dark green dragon. "You weren't kidding. You're a dragon."

No. I would never kid about this. She moved

107

around him and Devon spread his wings. They were green as well but more translucent, almost see through. *I can show all of myself to you, but I don't want to frighten you.*

"I don't have any idea, but I'm not afraid of you." He turned a little, his tail moving along the grass, and his back became sharp. Spikes as long as her arm just appeared there, and she reached out to touch one of them. They were sharp enough to cut her, and she took the small wound to her mouth.

I'm sorry, love. I should have warned you. Moving around his body after telling him she was fine, she saw that there were sharp razor like scales at his knees and elbows. His forehead was battle ready as well, she thought. Standing in front of him, she realized that he was taller, too, than his counterpart, and more than likely heavier. *What do you think? Do I make you tremble with fear?*

"Yes and no. I'm not afraid of you, as I said, but you are frightening. Do you fly much? I mean, do the people in the village see you?" He moved and his armor disappeared. His wings too curled around his body and he moved to circle her.

Some of them do. The staff does. As for flying, yes,

when it's cloudy or raining. It's harder to see me when there isn't a bright sun out. He stood in front of her again. *Would you like to see?*

"See?"

Before she could think what he was about, she found herself in his arms and soaring upward. His large claws were wrapped around her but it didn't hurt. Kelly was flying. Flying with her dragon mate.

The village looked so small from this height. And when some of the people came out of their homes and looked up at them, waving, Kelly waved back. It was strange knowing that she was held like this, by a creature that she hadn't believed in, but also it was exhilarating as well.

They flew up to the great mountains behind the castle, over the bay that she'd been to just a few days ago. Over fields and fields of planted pastures. Orchards of fruit trees. And when they came upon an area of sheep, Devon dipped them down close enough that it had them running for cover. Kelly was still laughing when he took them home and shifted to himself again.

"I've never done that before. Carried anyone with me to fly. But with you, I'd do it every day.

I love you so very much." Kelly hugged him back when he took her into his arms. And when he swung her around, her feet stretched out behind her, she laughed again. Kelly had never been this happy before.

"My lord." They both turned to see Benshaw. He was smiling and she felt like giving him a hug as well. "My lady, my lord, you have a visitor in the parlor. I think it's to do with your sister and mother, my lady."

"Whoever it is tell them that we've run away and you can't find us." He glanced at Devon then looked at her again. "I'm kidding. Do you know what this is about? Or can we guess."

"There was some damage done to his establishment. I do believe that you were told, sir?" Kelly looked at Devon when he said yes. "He said that he needed to speak with you about it."

"We'll be in shortly. Could you make sure that he has tea and some of those wonderful scones, please? I want to talk to my lady first." After Benshaw left them, she asked Devon what was going on. "Your sister was pissed that the store had refused to use the broken credit card. Then when he asked her to leave, she picked up one of his paintings and used it as a battering ram for other items in his store. Your mother tried to rob the till."

"Christ." He said nothing but watched her. "Are you sure you want to marry me? What if I turn out like them?"

"Never. But I would like to know what you'd like to do about this. I will pay for damages, that's a given, but I don't know what you want do to about Rachel and your mom." Neither did she and she said that to him. "They could do some serious jail time on this, depending on the amount of things broken. Theft isn't taken lightly here either."

"Nor at home." She looked at the great castle that she'd only seen from the bridge. It seemed so long ago now. "I'll take care of them if you can arrange to have them shipped home. Not first class nor on your plane. Cheapest way to go. Also, do you think you can loan me two thousand dollars? And someone to write up a contract that says that's all they'll ever get and that if they contact us again, we'll...I don't know. We'll do something to them."

"I can do that. And my money is yours." She wasn't going to argue that point right now, but they were going to have to talk when her family was taken care of. "What about them in jail? I think they can stay where they are if you like, or back here."

"Jail is where they deserve to be. Also, do you know how to send a voice mail to someone?" He said he could find out. "I have a confession from my sister that says she did the damage to my place. I don't want her to know what I'm doing, but I think the police would be interested to know who did it."

"I think I love the way you think. Now, one more thing before we go inside." He pulled her into his arms and kissed her. She felt melted, her body leaning into his for support, when he lifted his head. "Will you marry me? As soon as I can get it arranged?"

"Yes. Yes, I will." As they made their way into the house again, she thought of her vacation and the things she'd done. And now, to end it all, she was going to be the man-of-her-dreams' wife. Kelly was so happy; she was giddy with it.

CHAPTER 6

Rachel paced the small cell. Whatever reason they had for putting her in here, she was going to make them regret it. And her sister too. The nerve of her giving Rachel stolen credit cards so that she'd take the fall for her. As soon as the officer that had put them in here came down the little hall, she told him to get her sister.

"Lady Kelly is here with our lordship." And that shit was going to stop as well. "They would like for me to ask you if you are ready for them to speak to you. If not, they'll come back tomorrow."

"I'm not speaking to her." When he walked

away, Rachel sat down and looked over at her mom. "That'll have her come running. She hates it when we're mad at each other. But I have to make her see that she can't treat us this way all the time."

"That store was wrong to tell us that we couldn't spend our money there. I mean, it's not like Kelly isn't good for it. She does have a good job and all." Rachel nodded in total agreement. "When we all get home, I think we should make her get us all a bigger place. So you and I can have our own rooms. When we have all our pretties from here, I want to put them out so people can see them."

"I like that idea. I was also thinking about her accounts. The one at the bank that she never kept up with. Do you think we can get a credit card on one of those? That way as soon as she puts our money in there, we can have a kind of ding thing that lets us know." Her mom said she didn't know much about banks. "Me either, but we'll have Kelly make it work."

She wanted a cell phone too, one of the kind that Devon had. He could check his email and all kinds of crap on his. All she could do with the one she had was answer a call. She wasn't even able to take any decent pictures with it. As she sat there waiting for Kelly to come and beg her forgiveness, she started making a list of things that she was going to have Kelly get for them.

The new television had to be first. And not one of those little ones either. Rachel wanted one that hung on the wall and had all the stations on it. She wanted to be able to watch whatever she wanted all the time. And she wanted a credit card set up on the shopping stations. They had so many pretty things on there that would just make her day to have.

"You think they're talking things over?" Rachel got up to look down the hall to the door where the cop had disappeared when her mom spoke again. "She sure is taking her time about this. Like she's trying to teach us some kind of lesson."

"She's forever doing things like that. I have no idea why. I like things like I like them." Her mom said she did too. "I just don't understand her at times. Are you sure that she's really my sister? I mean, maybe they switched her up at birth. Wouldn't surprise me to find that out there is this person out there just as pretty as I am with the same needs and wants. Kelly is not nice."

She kept thinking of the account. That had only been the beginning of how Kelly had mistreated her. To think that Rachel had let her in on her plans to see the world, and had her sister take it out from under her like she'd not had her name on the account too. The money had been there, why not use it to make sure that they were ready to go on time? It was not like Kelly didn't have a way to keep adding to it. but she'd stopped doing that too.

"I should have looked for another passbook when I was snooping around her house. Why she feels the need to hide things from me is just crazy. It's not like she was using any of the things I sold. I mean, they didn't bring much anyway. I did her a favor in getting rid of them for her. If she hadn't put on her calendar that she was going away, then we wouldn't have been any the wiser." Her mother said that it was just like her to be all secretive and shit. "I know. It's like she never trusted us."

"What reason can she have for not trusting us? We didn't stop putting money in that account. We didn't leave us stranded at the airport with no clothing or tickets. We trusted her to do like she promised, and what did that get us? Nothing. I have said this a million times, she is the most ungrateful kid ever born." Rachel agreed.

"And why is everyone calling her a lady? She's nothing. Not even a pretty girl. I mean, she has lost all that weight, and I will not believe that she's not had any work done. Do you suppose that's why she didn't want us to go with her on our trip? Because she didn't want us to know about her plans? I bet you that's where all our money went too. Instead of in the account, she was paying someone off to suck her fat out." Rachel knew that was it. "I swear to you, Mom, she is going to pay every penny of my money back to me. I don't know how much she owes me, but she's gonna be paying me back for a long time."

When it was apparent that no one was coming down the hall right now, she sat down. The bed was lumpy and she wasn't sure where her mom was going to sleep if they ended up here overnight. But Rachel didn't think it would come to that. Kelly would get her head on straight and come get them. She'd better have some money on her too. There wasn't any way Rachel was leaving here without her things. Kelly owed her.

The door opened and closed again and Rachel didn't move. Kelly was going to have to beg her to listen to her after the way she'd treated her. But when a man stood there, another cop, he asked her if she wanted the food or not. All he had on him was two bags of fast food and two cans of soft drink.

"We'll be going out for dinner. Kelly is taking Mom and me out to that place down from the hotel." The cop said that Lady Kelly had gone home. "What do you mean, she's gone home? I didn't talk to her, she can't have left yet."

"You said that you weren't speaking to her and she left...she and his lordship." Rachel stood up and glared at the man. "Would you like this or not? Doesn't matter to me one way or the other."

"We're going out to dinner. I told Kelly about it and she'll come here to pick us up. And tell her to bring Mom and me something new to wear to the restaurant. We've made arrangements for the three of us to have dinner at six. She'll have to hurry now." The cop shoved the bags of food at her and put the cans on the floor. "When is she coming back to pick us up? When you talk to her, tell her not to forget money for the things we have at the shops."

He closed the door again and she sat down. The food smelled old and she opened it up to have a look at it. Fish sandwiches and fries? She wasn't going to spoil her dinner over something like that. Tossing it to the trash can, she did open one of the sodas up and drink it.

As soon as she was dressed up for their dinner, she was going to have to have her hair touched up again. There was no way she was going to be seen looking like a hobo. Kelly would have to pay for someone to come there when they were ready to go.

"That man, Devon, he's not a nice man, is he? I mean every time I tried to tell him the way he needed to do things, he just ignored me. I don't think I cared for him." Mom said she hadn't either. "He's a lot like Kelly too, did you notice? Always spouting about how I should do this or that. Why should I have to find a job? I hate working. And Kelly provides for us just fine."

"When she's not in a snit." That was true too. "She sure has been in those a lot lately. Like before she ran off with our money and you told her about the play we were to see. Remember that?"

119

"I do. All she had to do was go down to the ticket office and pay for them like I arranged for her to do. But not Kelly…she never does things like she's supposed to. We missed out on seeing that play because she decided that she needed something else. What could be more important than seeing a first run play like we planned?" Rachel felt her anger at Kelly rise up. "And when I told her how disappointed I was in her, she had the nerve to act like it wasn't any big deal for her to back out on that too. Like she didn't promise that she'd take care of it for us."

Kelly was acting all strange now too. Like whatever Rachel told her wasn't important. It was Devon, he was making her say these things. Kelly was too stupid to see that the man was coming between them, that he was trying to ruin their perfect family. When they got home and away from him, she'd have to have a long conversation with her sister and have her get her priorities straight again. Like doing the things for them that she'd promised.

When the lights suddenly snapped off in the hall, Rachel looked at her watch. There was no way it was after nine o'clock. Her sister had broken her promise again. This was just getting old. When you tell someone that you were taking them out to a really nice restaurant, then you should do it. And where was the pretty clothing and nice shoes to go with it? Kelly was going to have to make up for a lot of shit when they went home, and Rachel was going to make sure that she knew just how angry she was at her for breaking promises. Again.

~~~

Kelly followed Benshaw up the long hall. He'd been showing her around for nearly two hours and she was having a great time. And when she asked him a question about this or that, he took such pride in answering her that she had wanted to know it all. But he told her that this hall was the best as far as he was concerned.

"This is his lordship's mother. Lady Anna lived here before she wed, and this portrait of her was only brought out again after the ninth Marquess passed." Kelly stood in front of the large painting and thought that Devon looked a great deal like her. "There was no painting of her made when she was wed, but I do believe there are pictures of her at her wedding to him."

"Devon said he wasn't a nice man." She looked at Benshaw when he said nothing. "I'm sorry. I forget that you have some sort of code to live by. You must find it hard to talk to me when I'm such a dork."

"Not at all, my lady. We all find you refreshing and good for his lordship. He's been happy since you've come here." She nodded and turned to look at the painting again. "There in the corner, do you see the mark?"

She leaned closer to the corner of the painting where he'd indicated. The dragon was as big as her hand, but very small in comparison to the painting itself. And it was a blue dragon. She wanted to run her fingers over the beauty of the creature, and was just about to touch it when she felt heat coming from it. Finally, giving into temptation, she did touch it and felt the burn on her finger like she'd touched a hot flame. When she backed from the painting, her finger in her mouth, she was staring at it when the dragon came from the painting and stood in front of her.

"Stand very still, Kelly." She nodded at Devon's

voice when he spoke behind her. "Just let her... whatever she wants to do, let her."

"She's not big enough to eat me, is she?" Devon laughed and she turned to him. "That was in the painting until a minute ago, and now she's flying around like she's been alive all this time."

"She has been, I believe." When she flew in front of her again, Kelly backed up. She paced her, her beautiful wings flitting so quickly that she could feel the heat of them. "It's my mother's dragon, I think. I felt her, or something, and I came to find out what mischief you'd gotten into, only to find that you've awakened her other half. I have no idea how you've done it either."

"Oh my." When she heard Susanna speaking, Kelly started to turn to go to Devon but tripped. As she was falling, her arms flaying out to keep herself from harming herself, the dragon touched her. Kelly felt it all over her body. Then she was standing before her.

My lady. The dragon bowed low, her wings no longer moving now that she was standing before her. *I should like to see you stand up, if you please. To see into your eyes.*

123

"I think I like it just fine where I am." But Devon was there and he helped her stand up. He didn't leave her, as she was afraid he might, but put his arms around her waist and stood behind her. "How is it that you've come out of the painting?"

I was never a part of it. I have been.... When her ladyship was dying, she sent me away, to stay here in this picture to wait. Telling me that someday I'd be set free. I have been waiting and watching all this time for the meaning of her words to come to pass. The dragon moved closer to Kelly, her eyes seeming to bore into her head, and laughed. *You are more worthy than I ever thought of such a gift, my lady.*

"A gift from whom? And what is it you think I've done to be worthy of it?" The dragon looked down the hall toward Susanna. "You hurt her and I will kill you. Dragon or not, you won't hurt the most wonderful woman I've ever met."

The dragon turned to her then. *I should never hurt the one who brought me to life.* Kelly looked at Susanna to ask her how she'd done it. *Not like you think, my lady. But in that her dragon is mother to me.*

"Oh, I never.... I'm very sorry for what I said just now. I just wanted to keep her safe, that's all.

I've come to love her as a mom, and I don't want to lose her." The dragon smiled at her then. "You're very beautiful. I mean, I'm sure that you know that, but you're a lot like Lady Anna, aren't you?"

She was my other half. It occurred to her that she was having a conversation with a dragon and asked her how she was doing that. *When you touched me, you were harmed; nothing that has not healed, but we have a connection now. Much like the one that you have with Devon.*

"I don't know why you're here. I mean, I'm glad for it. Lady Susanna probably misses her daughter, and you can tell her things that she would love to know. But why now, why did you wake when I touched you?" She looked at Devon when he tightened his grip on her. "I think my mate would like to get to know you as well."

And he shall. If I have your permission. She was confused. Why would she need her permission to talk to Devon? *Because in order for him to know love like he deserves, you must become all that you can.*

"I thought I was." The dragon laughed. "I'm not sure why you need it, but if you wish to talk with Devon you have my permission. Just don't hurt him."

As you wish. The dragon flew up to the ceiling, the height of it dizzying when she saw the brightness of the dragon there. And when she started down, her wings back on her body, her face pointed at her, she thought her the most beautiful creature once again. Then Devon stepped back and she was standing alone.

The dragon's body slammed into her. Kelly staggered from the impact. When she felt herself falling, her body aching all over, she heard someone screaming, the sound of it echoing into her head, and realized it was her. Falling back to the floor, Kelly had a moment, just a small one, in which she thought that she was dead, that the very thing that she'd brought to life had killed her. Then as suddenly as she had begun hurting, the pain disappeared.

Her head was fuzzy—she felt like there was cotton between her ears—but she heard him, heard Devon speaking…but his words made no sense to her. When he touched his hands to her face, she tried harder to listen to him, but all she knew was that his mouth was moving but there was no sound.

Putting her hands over her ears, she curled into a ball and asked for a moment. At least she wanted to ask for it. As she lay there, things became clearer. The sounds were going in and out, and she started hearing the conversation going on around her.

"Can you hear me yet?" She nodded but lay very still when Devon spoke. "I'm not going to try and move you until you're ready. You've had something amazing happen, and I don't want to freak you out."

"Yes, because you telling me that, might just makes me calmer." He laughed and she looked up at him. "I think she tried to kill me. Where is she anyway? I'd like to have a little talk to her about giving permission and what that might mean to someone."

"She's here. With you." Kelly nodded. "My grandmother said that this has only happened once in all her life, but she's never witnessed it before."

Kelly saw him sit then, his legs stretched out by her, and she lifted her head slowly and laid it on his thigh. He touched her head with his long fingers and she felt better with the touch. Everything about her felt...wonderful now.

"I think I can get up now." He asked her for a little bit longer, that his heart was still racing. "That dragon, she hit me, didn't she? I think she might have broken me up a little too, but you healed me."

"She hit you, yes, but she didn't harm you. She became a part of you." She looked at him when what he said hit her. "My mother's dragon, she is now a part of you. It's called *a bheith ar cheann*. It means to become one. Grandmother said it wasn't practiced much, but when it was, the receiver of the dragon became as if she'd been born one."

"You mean that she, your mother's dragon, hit me, and that I'm now a dragon." He explained the hitting part. "So she flew into me. And through me to make me what you are."

"My mother knew about you." Kelly stood up. It was too much to be having this conversation on the floor. "You're not mad, are you? I mean, I can see why you would be. She did sort of trick you into.... Where are you going?"

"Outside. I want to see her." When she was nearly down the stairs, she saw Susanna. She'd been crying, and it hurt her in ways that she'd never felt for her own mom. "You knew this might happen?"

"No. Never in all my life. I was with her to the end, my darling daughter, and she said nothing to me. When you were resting, she told us that you were the one that would heal all wounds, and that Anna knew that you'd be a wonderful mate to her son."

Kelly hugged Susanna and told her that she was glad that she was there with them. But she moved out the door before Susanna could say anything, like she wanted her to give the dragon back to her daughter. Devon came out on the deck where she was.

"Can I fly?" He nodded, smiling at her. "And do all the things you can.... Hey, I just thought of something. Can we have sex as...? Eww. I'm your mom's dragon."

Devon laughed and sat on the stairs to the yard where she was now. "She's your dragon, Kelly. Not my mother's any longer. You might have a few of her memories, I don't know for sure, but your dragon is just that...yours."

Thinking of the beautiful dragon in the hall, Kelly only hoped that she'd be just as pretty. She knew what she looked like and didn't want the dragon to be ashamed for being a part of her. Then she felt her, the stirring along her skin, and let her take her.

"Christ." She looked at Devon and felt his love pour over her. He pulled out his cell phone and was pointing it at her before she figured out he was taking her picture. She wanted to see them, but also wanted to fly. Looking skyward, she thought about spreading her new wings there.

I don't know how to do it. She looked at him when he said nothing. *I'd like to fly, I really would, but I haven't any idea how to do it.*

"You just think of flying, love, and the dragon will do the rest. You should see you as I do now. The lady of the castle, the dragon of my heart." She turned and looked at him again. "If you'd like, I could come with you. I would very much like to fly with you."

Yes, please do. She watched him stand and come to her. When he was close enough that she could feel his heat, he shifted. His dragon was bigger than hers, by a lot, but she had no problem with that. He was hers, and Kelly was in love with both of them.

CHAPTER 7

Devon watched her carefully. She had taken to it like she had being lady of the castle; like she'd done it all her life. And when she moved over the town, everyone that could came out to see them, waving at their new lady and sending up cheers for them both. Devon asked her if she was ready to see the mountains.

Can we become human again? I mean, I love being this other me, but I'd like to touch you. I find that I need to touch you. He told her that he wanted her as well. Almost as soon as their feet touched the ground, she was her human self, but naked. "I need you."

When his dragon melted away from him,

Devon reached for Kelly. Her body was different now, stronger and warmer. He kissed her, telling her with his mouth how much he wanted to take her. Lifting her up, he felt her wrap her legs around him when he pressed her to the closest wall of stone. Letting her go, he stepped back from her and dropped to his knees in front of her.

Devon pulled her pussy to his mouth and sucked on her hard clit. She rode his mouth as he ate her, her juices hot now, much warmer than they had been before. As he devoured her, drinking her as quickly as she released, he fisted his cock to relieve some of the ache that he felt. Lifting up one of her legs, he put it on his shoulder and spread her nether lips wider. He watched her pussy tremble and he blew his breath over her.

She screamed out his name as she came for him. Her clit seemed to beg to be bitten, so he tasted her. And when she curled her fingers into his hair and pulled him tighter to her, Devon slid his hand up her thigh and pushed two of his fingers into her to bring her again.

"Fuck me." He watched her, looking up at her while he suckled at her pussy. "Please. Fuck me,

Devon. Hard. I need you to fuck me really hard."

He nearly tossed her to the ground, his body aching to fill her, to take her like he needed to. And when she spread her legs for him, showing him how ready she was for him, Devon leaned over her and slammed his cock as deeply and as hard as he could.

Kelly screamed again, her voice echoing around them, bouncing off the stone of the mountains and back to them. When he pulled from her and filled her again, he nearly came when she begged him to take her harder, to give her what she needed. Filling her again, this time holding her body to his, Devon pounded her as hard as he could until she screamed again and bit him.

Stars…there were stars in his vison he was so blown away by the release that took him. As he pounded more, emptying everything that he had into her, she came three more times, taking him with her each time she did. When she was as limp as he felt, he dropped over her and rolled to his back, his body too spent to even make sure that they were safe where they were. Sleep took him.

When he woke he was alone, but he knew that

she was close and turned to his side to see her. She was sitting by one of the trees with a small circle of flowers around her. He sat up when he realized where she was. Dressing, because she was dressed, he made his way to her, careful not to disturb the faerie circle that she was in.

"I've been talking to my dragon. She told me to sit here and that we could talk. I didn't know what this was until they came out to see me." She nodded to the little faeries that he'd seen before. They bowed when he nodded to them and he looked at Kelly again. "They said they were to serve me."

"All faerie are for us. We serve each other." She nodded and smiled at him. "Did she tell you the meaning of the circle that you're in?"

"Yes. There is a dragon on the other side. That when they died, someone put their ashes here and a garden, this garden, was made to protect them. There is but a single flower that can close it off to all who would harm them. She said that you have it. And so long as I don't call to her, she won't come to me. But that if I need her, she'll be there. She'll come to me in the form of a faerie." Devon nodded and opened his hand, and the necklace that had been his since he'd been born was there. He put it out in his hand for her to take. "You don't have to give it to me, Devon. It's yours."

"I wish for you to have it." He sat up and put it over her head, the chain changing to fit her, and he sat back down. "When a dragon dies, he turns to ash, much like a vampire but not quite the same way. Dragon ash has special powers that when it is touched by someone that loved the dragon, they are forever touched by his magic. This flower and the ash within are that of my great grandparents. They are both on the other side of this garden."

"You never touched the ash or met them." He shook his head and told her that they were both gone before his mother had been born. "I'm sorry about that. I'm sure they were very nice people."

"Yes, from what I heard, they were wonderful people." He watched her as she sat there, the flowers, an offering from the faeries, in her lap. He picked one up and handed it to the faerie to let them start their work. "When a dragon male finds his mate, another dragon, there is a great celebration. Many faeries come from everywhere for their coming together. The faeries bring with them magic, magic that they share with the couple. The magic can produce a child should they like."

"You mean for us to have a baby?" He nodded but said nothing. "This celebration, she mentioned that it happens when the trees were ready to open, the flowers to bloom. I take it that it's sort of like a birth of a great many things."

"It is. But should you like to wait, then we can." She watched the faeries as they wove the flowers into a long chain, one that Kelly would wear to their wedding. "I'd very much like for you to marry me. Now, today if you'll have me."

"I will." He nodded, unsure of her mood at the moment. "I would like to have a child with you. Many if you don't mind. But we have to deal with my mom and sister first."

"We can do that now if you want." She nodded but continued to watch the faeries. "What is it, love? You seem so...I don't know, but sad for some reason."

"Your mother was poisoned. It's what killed her. She was given dragons breath, a flower known to poison only your kind and the faeries that surround you. Your father fed it to her himself, not trusting the staff to do it for him. He had tried to order them to kill you off as well, knowing when you were born that you were a dragon." Devon said nothing as he listened to her. "He saw your mark. And when he did, he went into such a rage that he tried to stab you with a blade. But you had protection. You've always been protected; did you know that?"

"Yes. First it was Benshaw, then it was his grandson. They're faeries as well." She nodded. "Do you know how he was killed? My father, do you know what happened to him?"

"Your dragon, he killed him when your father meant to beat him from you." Devon felt his heart break, knowing that she'd hate him now. "I don't. Hate you, I mean. I love you, and am glad your dragon ended your nightmare."

"No one knows what he did to me. Benshaw did. My father hated me. I never knew that he understood what I was." He looked down over the fields that they'd flown over, the homes with the people that had come to mean more to him now more than ever. Kelly had shown him what love really was. "When he was dead, I called to the staff. Once they confirmed what I already knew, the police were called and he was taken away. No one asked me what had happened. There were no questions as to why he'd fallen. No one, not a single person, seemed to care any more than I did that my father was dead."

"They knew even then, I'd bet, that everyone, you included, would be safer after he was gone." Devon nodded and laid back on the grass. "This is so peaceful here. Do you suppose that's why your grandparents picked this place?"

"I would say that back when they came here, there wasn't even a town to speak of." He sat up when she stood and stepped out of the ring. "We must go and deal with your family. Are you ready?"

"No. But I'm more ready today than I was a week ago. I don't think they're going to like me overly.... Well, they're not going to like me at all after this." He wanted to say good, but it was her mom and sister. Laughing, she made her way to him and wrapped her arms around him. "My dragon, take me home."

~~~

Rachel and her mom were taken to a conference

room. It was drab and needed to be updated too. There wasn't even a vending machine that had anything good in it, and no matter how many times she told them to charge it to her sister, they would not give her anything from it.

"This shit is going to have to be fixed. Kelly should know better than to leave us here and not provide for us." Her mom nodded. "We didn't even have a decent bed to sleep in. And no television at all. Christ, you'd think we'd done something wrong."

They both looked at the officer who had walked in the room with them. Rachel asked him where their breakfast was. "And not that crap you brought us all ready. You made us miss our dinner out with Kelly last night, and I won't have you making us anything nasty. I'll have an omelet with bacon on the side and coffee. Not that dark stuff you brought us yesterday."

"Tea. It was tea. And I'm not bringing you breakfast. You had it." She told him she had not. "You did. I brought you sausage and bean with toast."

"We didn't like the way it looked, and you

served it on paper plates. That is not the way we wanted it. Now, I want an omelet with bacon on the side. Crispy. I want—"

"Her ladyship asked that you write down what you want before you go home that you'd like to take. One or two things, like souvenirs. She said that you're leaving today, thank the good Lord. And that she wanted you to know that your things are packed up too and ready at the airport." Rachel took the notebook and pen and felt like this was the way things should have been from the start. "And do not be asking me for breakfast again. You didn't eat what was served, and that's all there will be until noontime." After he left, she looked at her mom.

"I'm glad to see that she's finally coming around. I have to tell you, Mom, I despaired of her ever getting with the program. To think that she has been treating us badly all this time, and it took us staying away from her for a day for her to understand how much she needs us."

"You should write that down. That she needs us. And that we'll suffer through letting her stay in the apartment with us. You tell her that we want a bedroom apiece. I don't want to have to share." Rachel nodded. "And then you tell her that we need her to set up an account with our names on it, not hers. No more of her just taking our money whenever she feels like it."

"And no more trips for her. When we plan something, we'll think about letting her go with us. She'll have to work some overtime I guess, but that'll be fine. With her gone all the time, you and I can have parties. Credit cards...we need them with our names on them. Ones without limits too. No more of her dictating how much we spend."

Rachel was writing things down as fast as she and her mom could think of them. Changes were needed when they got home. And the first one was that she was going to have to start putting money back in that account. Rachel did note that she'd only take from it when it was necessary. She simply wasn't going to have her nails and hair done at different times from now on. It made her feel unbalanced, and she hated that. When the door opened, she looked up at the gorgeous woman who stood there. Then Devon.

"Where is Kelly? She's supposed to come here

and we're going to give her this list of things that we want." The woman said she was Kelly. Rachel stared at her. "What did you do? You can't have had your face and body redone. I looked into it… you're all bandaged up for a long time after. What happened to you?"

"I fell in love." Kelly sat down and so did Devon. "Now, what is it you want before you leave here?"

Rachel looked at her notes and then back at her sister. "I'm glad that you're finally doing things the right way. You should know that Mom and I understand that you've been under a lot of stress, working as hard as you do. And we've decided that we should all live in the same apartment so that you don't have to give us money for rent all the time. Also, we'd like a place that is bigger than the one you had before. Mom and I don't want to have to share your bed, so we need you to find us one that has two bedrooms in it." Kelly asked her where she was supposed to sleep in this apartment. "Oh, on the couch. But not in our rooms. We need to be able to have some privacy and to put our things where we want them. You can clean up after us but not

142

move our things. That's gotta be set in stone."

"I see. And who pays the rent on this apartment?" Rachel just stared at her. "I see. I would. And I'm assuming the utilities as well?"

"Well, yes. It would be your place. Kelly, what would we do if you didn't have the power paid? We couldn't watch television, nor could we see in the dark. You would need to get either a second job right away or work a lot of overtime. We have other things that you have to get for us as well."

"When I asked them to give you this paper, it was for you to see if you wanted to take home a tea cup or a glass globe. Not make demands on me." Rachel just waved her off. Kelly was forever getting things wrong. "I'm not getting things wrong, Rachel. I want you to know that I'm not going to pay for any of this either."

"That account that you took all our money from? We need that filled up again. All the time. And when we run short, you should have money at the house for us. Mom and I were thinking that you could put in a nice safe and have ready cash in there for us. You never know when there is something special we'll want." Rachel looked at her notes.

143

"Credit cards too, with our names on them. And no limit or anything on it that says we have to call you before we can use it. The last time I took your cards from your purse, the man said that I couldn't use them without proper identification. I tried to tell him that you were good for it, but he just wouldn't use that. I don't want to be embarrassed like that again."

"Yes, we don't want you inconvenienced when you steal my credit cards and can't use them." Rachel smiled at her. "I wasn't being serious, Rachel. You stole my cards. It's only right that you shouldn't be able to use them."

"That makes no sense whatsoever, Kelly. You're just being selfish. Anyway. When we get home I want you to pay me back for all the money you stole from us to take this big vacation that I planned out." Kelly huffed at her. "Well, you did run off without taking us with you. And after everything I did for you, too."

"What did you do? Other than take my money that I had worked hard for and saved up. Do you know how much I had to give up to put that money in there?" Rachel started to speak but was cut off.

"You took it all. Left a single dollar in there like you were taunting me."

"I would never taunt you. They wouldn't let me take the last dollar. Something about having both of us sign for the account to be closed. And then you just stopped putting money in there. And I did help you out, Kelly. Did you forget that I gave you a list for things Mom and I would need? Didn't I tell you about the camera that we wanted to take? And what did you do? Not only did you not buy us anything at all, you took the money for our vacation and went on it all by yourself. You can be the most selfish person I know sometimes."

Kelly stood up and Rachel could see that she was angry. Well, so was she. Why did she forever have to be telling her sister how she had wronged them? And how she'd taken their money. For Christ's sake, it was a joint account, wasn't it? The money was hers too.

"Your flight leaves in one hour. Your tickets are at the counter and so are your passports. You'll need those to get your luggage put on the plane. When you arrive home, there will be a car to take you to your own place. The moment that you set foot out of this jail, you will not have contact with me again. As far as I'm concerned, we're finished."

"But you're going to be living with us, so us not seeing you isn't going to happen. Unless you're working all the time. Which I don't see how you're not going to be with all the money that you owe us. Not to mention keeping the bills up."

"The police in Ohio know that you burned my apartment and why you did it." Rachel asked her why that was important. "Because you did damage to a place that wasn't yours."

"It was yours, so who cares what I did to it? And if that's something else you're going to have to pay for, that comes out of your pocket, not mine. I have enough expenses, what with having my hair done and going shopping for new clothing. You should have taken better care that no one could get in." Rachel looked at her list and it was snatched away from her by Kelly. "Yes, you should more than likely keep it. That way when you take care of something, you can mark it off. But leave it where I can find it. I might think of something else."

Kelly and Devon started for the door and Rachel stood up. They were leaving? Now? She'd not even gone over the last five pages of things that Kelly was going to need to take care of. But when Devon turned to her, she had a feeling that he wasn't going to be as nice about things as she'd been. He was just rude and mean.

"You're going to be arrested as soon as you get home. I thought you should know that. And the demands that you made on your sister? They're not going to happen either. She is going to become my wife in a few days, and the only way you're going to get to see her is if you save your money and come here. And we all know that isn't going to happen." Rachel asked him why he was marrying Kelly and not someone pretty. "She's lovely, and you saw it too. Don't contact us again or I will take measures to have your miserable lives become hell."

When he left, Rachel realized that Kelly hadn't taken her list. She'd just take it with her and give it to her when they got home. This was just silly. Things were going to be just fine and back to normal when they got back to Ohio. Someplace where Devon wasn't. He was a bad influence on her sister, and Rachel was going to have to suffer through doing something else for Kelly.

"Do you suppose she really isn't going to come home with us? What will we do, Rach? She won't be able to put money in our accounts if she's not at home working." Rachel patted her mom on the hand, telling her that things would be just fine. "I don't know, Rach. She looked like she was pretty happy here."

"She needs us. Didn't we prove that when we stayed here last night and not with her? Yes, she'll come around."

Rachel felt something she'd never felt before, doubt. It was the strangest feeling to have thoughts that her sister might not want to do the things that they wanted her to. Then she smiled. Kelly would do it; she might fuss a lot, but she'd do it. She was her sister, after all.

"Your ride is here." Rachel smiled at her mom when the officer came to get them. "Everything is set up at the airport for you."

"See, I told you she'd come around. I just knew she wasn't serious. Kelly can be cruel when she wants, but she always does what is.... What is this?" The car was old and beaten up. Not the limo that they'd been using while there. "I want the big car to take us. This isn't what Kelly said she was going to do for us. Don't make me have to call her and have this taken care of."

"Get in or I'm going to shove you in the back of the cruiser and take you there myself." Rachel started to argue but decided for now she'd do what this brute told her. As they were riding to the airport, she tried to call her sister.

"They're saying that the number is no longer in service. She didn't pay the bill again. I tell you, she needs a keeper. How does she expect me to call her when we need things if she doesn't keep up with her bills? I do hope she doesn't try this when we get home. I won't have it." Rachel was getting really sick of having to do everything all the time. "As soon as we get home, I'm going to put her on a budget. She'll turn her money over to us and then we'll get things done correctly."

Rachel was so upset when they were seated on the plane that she could hardly contain herself. Not only did they not have seats in the front of the plane, there wasn't a menu for them either. They got no blankets, and the waitress told her to sit down and buckle so many times that Rachel was

149

tempted to just call her sister and demand that she get them into someone better. But her phone was no longer working either.

"She might not have remembered to pay the bill on our phone either. I know that I told her several times that it was due. I tell you, Mom, things are going to have to change when we get home. A lot." But when the plane took off without Kelly, she wondered what was going on. There wasn't any way that Kelly would have a better seat on another plane. It wasn't very nice of her if she did. Rachel pulled out her paper again and started making a list. This one her sister was going to have to abide by. "She's out of control. We're going to have to bring her home and have a talk with her. Make her understand that she can't be doing this any longer. We have needs and she's not meeting them."

The police waiting for her at the airport in Ohio was the final straw. Kelly was officially no longer her sister. She looked at her mom as she was being dragged away.

"Call Kelly. Tell her that I'm disappointed in her and that she needs to stop this lesson learning all together. If she doesn't take care, I'm going to have to cut her off. Then what will she do?"

"Rachel Dalton, you're under arrest for arson, breaking and entering. Thief—" She kicked out at the man and demanded that she be set free. He just slammed her against the car hood and held her there.

"It's all Kelly's fault. She should have had a better lock on her door, and if she hadn't been so selfish and hidden her money from me, then I'd not have to take her things and sell them."

She was being put into another cell in another jail when she realized something. Kelly wasn't coming back. She wasn't going to pay for her a new apartment, and there wasn't going to be any new things. Damn it all to hell, her sister was the meanest person in the world.

EPILOGUE

"I now pronounce you man and wife." Kelly kissed Devon when he pulled her to him. The wedding, like their lives together so far, was perfect. She looked out over the people who had come out to see them wed and smiled at them. The cheers were wonderful and the faeries dropped flowers over her and Devon as they made their way around to the villagers.

They'd been married in the field behind the castle. The setting had been beautiful and the weather had not failed them either. As they were hugged and congratulated, she thought of the conversation that she'd had with Mr. Bigalow just yesterday. She'd called him to let him know that she wasn't returning and that she'd paid him for the next year in rent so that he could find another tenant. And Devon had paid for the damages done to his apartment building.

"She's not right in the head, they're saying." She knew that. It had taken her a bit to figure it out, but she knew now that Rachel had some problems. "They found her not fit to stand trial, which in a way is good. She's been spouting off some things that would get herself in trouble if only half were true."

"I think they all might be, don't you?" He laughed. "I'm sorry about everything, Mr. Bigalow. I really am. Maybe someday you and your family could come for a visit. I'd love to show you around."

"You're happy, and I have to tell you, that tickles me like you were my own daughter. It really does. To be marrying, and a big deal too. And living in a pretty castle. You were sweet to send us photos. I tell you, I thought you were meant for bigger things, and you did it. Lady of the castle, you are." She had laughed, feeling really good about talking to him. "I have contacted some people like you asked for your momma. She's been staying in the apartment that your sister was at with her. They might be having to take her away too, I'm thinking. Poor thing keeps going on and on about.... Well, you're better off where you are. Not here with the two of them. They weren't fit to be family and you're better off, like I said."

Her mom had been telling everyone that her daughter Rachel was her only child, and that she'd had another one but she was dead to her. Their rent hadn't been paid in over six months, nor had any of their utilities. The day after tomorrow, if not sooner, her mom was going to be removed from the place and taken to a nursing home. Devon had wanted to pay the rent for her, but it would just start over again. It was best, she knew, to just be finished with them.

"A bride should not be frowning on her wedding day." Kelly looked over at Susanna and smiled. "You are so beautiful, my child. And I never would have imagined anyone more suited to wear the crown than you are."

Kelly touched her fingers to the bejeweled

crown that had been a gift to her from Devon just that morning. He told her that he'd wanted to give it to her sooner, but he didn't want her to freak out.

"When do you leave?" Susanna told her tonight. "I love that you're going on a long cruise, but I will miss you terribly."

"And I you." Kelly put her hand over her still flat belly. "I'll be here in time for the babe to be born. I'm so excited to be a great grandma. I'll be sending things home for you all the time while I'm gone. To think it only took a pretty girl from Ohio to make me the happiest woman in the world."

"And it only took a large dragon to do the same for me." Kelly hugged Susanna. "I have a favor to ask of you. I've spoken to Devon and he thinks.... Well, if you won't mind, I'd very much like to call you Grandmother as well. I know that I'm not really your gra—"

"Oh child, you have done so much for this poor old woman." She hugged her again and Kelly felt her eyes fill with tears. They did that a lot; her body seemed to overreact to the strangest things and she'd be sobbing. She looked at Devon when she felt his support. "He loves you very much. You know that, don't you?"

"Yes. Because I love him as well." She looked at her grandma now. "I don't know what to do to be a parent. I mean, love the baby and keep it safe, I got that part, but to raise a dragon, I don't have a clue."

"You will do fine. Better than fine, you'll be perfect at it." Kelly nodded, trying not to cry again. "I have a gift for you. It's not much, but I thought you should have it."

The ring was laying in the palm of Susanna's hand and Kelly looked without touching it. It was only a ring in the sense that it was round and fit on someone's finger. But it was so much more.

"It was my mothers. And hers before her. And so on and so on. It should have gone to my daughter on her wedding day, but she didn't want it. Well, she did, but she said for me to keep it for a little while longer. I think now she was afraid that her husband wouldn't allow her to wear it. It turned out she was right not to have taken it. I can now give it to you."

Kelly picked the ring up carefully and looked at it. It was a dragon. His tail wrapped around the gold of the base, and his mouth held a diamond that looked as big as the end of her thumb. When she slipped it on her finger, she felt the power of it roll over her. Kelly looked at her grandmother.

"What was that?" Susanna only laughed and hugged her again. "That was amazing. It was magical, wasn't it? Something in the ring was given to me, right?"

"Yes." She asked her what it was. "I'm not sure. It's different for each woman in the family. When Devon's mother just tried it on, she received the gift of sight. For my other daughter, the gift was being able to make herself invisible. For you? Who knows? Nothing about you has been by the books since I've met you. I'll be excited to see what powers you derive from this." When she kissed her again, Kelly knew that she was leaving them. "I have to go into town for a bit. Say good-bye to some friends, then on to the airport. You call out to me should you need me, and I will do the same."

Then she was gone. Kelly sat down on the chair and watched the people. She was glad now that she'd taken the vacation of a lifetime, because it had truly become just that. A wonderful adventure that had ended happily ever after for her.

Before You Go...

HELP AN AUTHOR

write a review

THANK YOU!

Share your voice and help guide other readers to these wonderful books. Even if it's only a line or two your reviews help readers discover the author's books so they can continue creating stories that you'll love. Login to your favorite retailer and leave a review. Thank you.

Kathi Barton, winner of the Pinnacle Book Achievement award as well as a best-selling author on Amazon and All Romance books, lives in Nashport, Ohio with her husband Paul. When not creating new worlds and romance, Kathi and her husband enjoy camping and going to auctions. She can also be seen at county fairs with her husband who is an artist and potter.

Her muse, a cross between Jimmy Stewart and Hugh Jackman, brings her stories to life for her readers in a way that has them coming back time and again for more. Her favorite genre is paranormal romance with a great deal of spice. You can visit Kathi online and drop her an email if you'd like. She loves hearing from her fans. aaronskiss@gmail. com.

Follow Kathi on her blog: http://kathisbartonauthor. blogspot.com/